MANIAC MARTIANS

MAROONED

IN

MASSACHUSETTS

Here's what readers from around the country are saying about Johnathan Rand's *AMERICAN CHILLERS:*

"I have read every single one of your books, and they are all AWESOME!"

-Ashley Y., age 12, California

"Thank you so much for coming to our school! The assembly was funny! I thought you were going to be really scary, but you weren't."

-Aaron P., age 11, Ohio

"I bought a pair of googly glasses from your website and I wear them everywhere. They are so cool!"

-James T., Age 8, Texas

"I just read VICIOUS VACUUMS OF VIRGINIA and it really creeped me out! It's my favorite book!"

-Samantha N., Age 11, Virginia

"Thank you so much for writing American Chillers. It's my favorite series in the whole world."

-Sean C., Age 9, Indiana

"My mom says the cover of DANGEROUS DOLLS OF DELAWARE really freaks her out. I read it and the story was even freakier than the cover!"

-Amber T., age 10, New York

"Our teacher read KREEPY KLOWNS OF KALAMAZOO to us, and it was great. Everyone in my class is in love with your books!"

-Payton K., Age 10, Michigan

"How come you always end every chapter at a good part? It drives me crazy because I have to keep reading to find out what happened!"

-Shannon L., Age 12, Colorado

"My family and I went to Chillermania and you were there with all three of your dogs! It was the best day of my life!"

-Michael R., Age 10, Michigan

"I just started reading your books and I love them! I'm going to read your whole series!"

-Sandra B., Age 9, Mississippi

"I read your books under the covers with a flashlight every night. They give me nightmares, but I love every book!"

-Robbie H., age 10, Oregon

"I told my brother I was going to send in my Chiller Blurb and tell you how much I love your books, but he says that you won't print it. Will you print my Chiller Blurb to prove my brother wrong? P.S: He loves your books just as much as I do."

-Garrett G., age 11, Arizona

"You came to our school last year and were really funny! Everyone in our school wants you to come back!"

-Maria F., age 8, Delaware

"I got five of your books for my birthday, and they were all autographed by you! Thank you so much! It was the best birthday gift EVER!"

-Paul D, age 10, North Dakota

"I can't wait to read OGRES OF OHIO! That's where I live! My dad thinks the title is funny, and he says that he's the REAL Ogre of Ohio!"

-Erin T., age 11, Ohio

"You are my favorite author! I can't believe you've written so many books! Do you wear those creepy glasses when you write your books? Do they help you make your books even scarier?"

-Brad S., age 10, South Carolina

"I just found out that you're going to write a book for every state! How long is it going to take you to do that? Please hurry up, because I can't wait to read all of them!"

-Robyn W., age 13, Maine

Got something cool to say about Johnathan Rand's books? Let us know, and we might publish it right here! Send your short blurb to:

Chiller Blurbs
281 Cool Blurbs Ave.
Topinabee, MI 49791

Other books by Johnathan Rand:

Michigan Chillers:

#1: Mayhem on Mackinac Island
#2: Terror Stalks Traverse City
#3: Poltergeists of Petoskey
#4: Aliens Attack Alpena
#5: Gargoyles of Gaylord
#6: Strange Spirits of St. Ignace
#7: Kreepy Klowns of Kalamazoo
#8: Dinosaurs Destroy Detroit
#9: Sinister Spiders of Saginaw
#10: Mackinaw City Mummies
#11: Great Lakes Ghost Ship
#12: AuSable Alligators
#13: Gruesome Ghouls of Grand Rapids
#14: Bionic Bats of Bay City
#15: Calumet Copper Creatures

American Chillers:

#1: The Michigan Mega-Monsters
#2: Ogres of Ohio
#3: Florida Fog Phantoms
#4: New York Ninjas
#5: Terrible Tractors of Texas
#6: Invisible Iguanas of Illinois
#7: Wisconsin Werewolves
#8: Minnesota Mall Mannequins
#9: Iron Insects Invade Indiana
#10: Missouri Madhouse
#11: Poisonous Pythons Paralyze Pennsylvania
#12: Dangerous Dolls of Delaware
#13: Virtual Vampires of Vermont
#14: Creepy Condors of California
#15: Nebraska Nightcrawlers
#16: Alien Androids Assault Arizona
#17: South Carolina Sea Creatures
#18: Washington Wax Museum
#19: North Dakota Night Dragons
#20: Mutant Mammoths of Montana
#21: Terrifying Toys of Tennessee
#22: Nuclear Jellyfish of New Jersey
#23: Wicked Velociraptors of West Virginia
#24: Haunting in New Hampshire
#25: Mississippi Megalodon
#26: Oklahoma Outbreak
#27: Kentucky Komodo Dragons
#28: Curse of the Connecticut Coyotes
#29: Oregon Oceanauts
#30: Vicious Vacuums of Virginia

American Chillers (cont'd)

#31: The Nevada Nightmare Novel
#32: Idaho Ice Beast
#33: Monster Mosquitoes of Maine
#34: Savage Dinosaurs of South Dakota
#35: Maniac Martians Marooned in Massachusetts

Freddie Fernortner, Fearless First Grader:

#1: The Fantastic Flying Bicycle
#2: The Super-Scary Night Thingy
#3: A Haunting We Will Go
#4: Freddie's Dog Walking Service
#5: The Big Box Fort
#6: Mr. Chewy's Big Adventure
#7: The Magical Wading Pool
#8: Chipper's Crazy Carnival
#9: Attack of the Dust Bunnies from Outer Space!
#10: The Pond Monster
#11: Tadpole Trouble

Adventure Club series:

#1: Ghost in the Graveyard
#2: Ghost in the Grand
#3: The Haunted Schoolhouse

For Teens:

PANDEMIA: A novel of the bird flu and the end of the world
(written with Christopher Knight)

American Chillers Double Thrillers:

Vampire Nation &
Attack of the Monster Venus Melon

#35: Maniac Martians Marooned in Massachusetts

Johnathan Rand

An AudioCraft Publishing, Inc. book

Book storage and warehouses provided by Chillermania!©
Indian River, Michigan

American Chillers #35: Maniac Martians
Marooned in Massachusetts
ISBN 13-digit: 978-1-893699-70-0

Librarians/Media Specialists:
PCIP/MARC records available **free of charge** at
www.americanchillers.com

Cover illustration by Dwayne Harris
Cover layout and design by Sue Harring

Printed in USA

Maniac
Martians
Marooned
in
Massachusetts

VISIT CHILLERMANIA!

WORLD HEADQUARTERS FOR BOOKS BY JOHNATHAN RAND!

CHILLERMANIA!

**I-75 Exit 313
then south
1 mile!**

Visit the HOME for books by Johnathan Rand! Featuring books, hats, shirts, bookmarks and other cool stuff not available anywhere else in the world! Plus, watch the American Chillers website for news of special events and signings at *CHILLERMANIA!* with author Johnathan Rand! Located in northern lower Michigan, on I-75! Take exit 313 . . . then south 1 mile! For more info, call (231) 238-0338. And be afraid! Be veeeery afraaaaaaiiiid . . . .

What I'm going to tell you is a story about Martians.

That's right.

Alien beings from Mars, one of the closest planets to Earth.

Now, you might think that this is a science fiction story, and that's partially true.

But for the most part, it's a horror story. A nightmare in real life, a terrifying experience that nearly cost the lives of me, my sister, and my friend one awful summer in Massachusetts.

But I'll also say this: if we hadn't stopped the Martians, they might have gone on to take over the entire state, then the country, and, quite possibly, the world.

So, you might say that we're heroes, and that alone makes me feel kind of proud. Oh, no one knows we're heroes, and we don't care. We're just glad that we did what we did, that we acted in time to save ourselves . . . let alone the entire human race.

My name is Damon Lewis, and I live in Boston, Massachusetts. I am 11 years old and going into fifth grade. I have a sister named Tracy, and she is one year younger than me. She's going into fourth grade. We get along fairly well, for the most part.

And up until one particular vacation last summer, I would have to say that my life was relatively boring. That's not to say that I don't have any fun. I have some great friends, and I love lots of things like sports, video games, and being outdoors. I think I like many of the things most kids my age do.

And one thing I look forward to every year

is our family vacation. Each year, we go somewhere different. One year we went to Disney World in Florida, and it was awesome! Another year, we went to Cedar Point in Ohio, and that was a lot of fun, too.

However, last summer, we decided to stay in our home state of Massachusetts to explore some of the places that we hadn't yet visited.

One of those places is called October Mountain State Forest. It's on the eastern side of Massachusetts and about a two and a half hour drive from our home in Boston. Dad told me all about it one morning during breakfast.

"You'll love it, Damon," he said to me as he placed his cup of coffee on the table. He had a map spread out before him, and he pointed to a particular spot with his index finger. "It's the biggest State Forest in Massachusetts, and there are miles and miles of hiking trails. You and Tracy are going to have the time of your lives."

And for the most part, my dad was right: Tracy and I, along with a friend that we met at the campground, Amber Duncan, would have the time of our lives. We just didn't know that having the time of our lives would also lead to an incredible discovery . . . and the most terrifying day we'd ever experienced.

On the day we left for vacation, we got a late start, because Dad couldn't find the car keys. He and Mom hunted all over for them. He was getting pretty angry, too. Dad gets mad when he loses things. One time, he forgot where he placed his wallet, and he tore the house apart looking for it. Of course, his wallet was in the exact place he'd left it: on the seat of the car in the garage. Still, he claimed he hadn't left it there and thought that someone else must've taken it to the car on purpose. Crazy.

Anyway, after about an hour of searching for the keys, guess what? Dad found them right where he had left them. They were on the mantle over the fireplace. I had no idea why he'd put them there, but being that he was the last one to drive the car, he was the most obvious one to have put them there.

Our drive was going to take us a couple of hours. For the most part, it was pretty boring. I played a video game while Tracy read a book. We got into an argument about something, and my dad, who was still angry from getting a late start, got mad at us.

"Do you want me to turn this car around?" he said as he looked up at the rearview mirror. Tracy had just slapped me on the shoulder, and I slapped her shoulder in return.

"Because I will," Dad continued. "Don't make me turn this car around, because I'll do it in a heartbeat."

The rest of the trip was silent. I didn't pay any attention to Tracy, and she paid no attention to me. I just played my game and caught glimpses of road signs as we traveled on Interstate 90. Once in a while, Mom would say something about our vacation and how fun it was going to be to stay in a campground instead of a hotel.

I was looking forward to that, too. Sure, I enjoyed staying in hotels when we went on vacation, but it wasn't very often that we went camping. I was looking forward to having a campfire, roasting marshmallows after dark, and helping Dad cook breakfast over the fire in the morning. I'd even bought a new pocket knife at a sporting goods store, and I couldn't wait to use it. There were a lot of things I was looking forward to . . . but getting attacked by Martians wasn't one of them.

I know it sounds crazy and unbelievable, and I wouldn't blame anyone if they didn't believe me.

Still, it happened, and to this day, I feel very lucky to be alive.

It took us longer than expected to get to our campsite, because Dad took a wrong turn, and we got lost. Dad said that the road he was taking was a shortcut to the State Forest campground, but as it turned out, it took us nearly sixty miles in another direction. We had to go all the way back and get on Interstate 90 again. Dad went on and on about how there 'used to be a shortcut, back in the good old days,' that they 'must have changed the route.'

    I thought the whole thing was kind of funny,

but I didn't say anything. I didn't want him mad at me!

So, by the time we got to October Mountain State Forest, it was already getting dark. And by the time we got around to putting up our tents, the stars were out. Dad and Mom had a large tent where they would sleep, and Tracy and I had a smaller, two-person tent that we set up next to theirs.

There were others in the campground, too. Some people had tents, while others had big campers and recreational vehicles. We could see campfires glowing in the early night and could smell the crisp, punky odor of wood smoke.

And I must admit: I really *was* excited. The last time we had used the tent, I'd set it up in our backyard. I had a friend over, and we stayed up really late, telling ghost stories.

But that really wasn't camping. Now, we were a long way from home in a place we'd never been before. I was excited about exploring the area and seeing some new things.

The next morning, Dad was in a much better mood. He was making breakfast over an open fire, and I awoke to the fantastic smells of scrambled eggs and bacon. The sun was already up, and it was a beautiful morning. I dressed, found my pocket knife, stuffed it into my pocket, and went outside into the fresh, cool morning air. Tracy awoke a few minutes later, and she came out of the tent in her pajamas, her hair all messy and tangled.

After breakfast, Dad sent me on an errand.

"Damon?" he said. He was holding an empty plastic gallon water jug in each hand.

"Yeah?"

"Will you take these over to the water spigot and fill them up?" he asked.

"Sure," I replied. I dried off my hands, took the water jugs from Dad, and set out across a small field, winding around other campsites, making my way toward a couple of small restrooms. Near the restrooms was a watering station, and there was a girl about my age doing the same thing I was about to do: filling up jugs of water. When she saw me coming, she smiled.

"I'll be done in just a second," she said as I approached. "Actually, I've been going slow, because I know that as soon as I get back to our campsite, my parents are going to put me to work again. I'm trying to kill some time."

I put my empty jugs on the ground. "Take your time," I replied. "I'm in no rush." Then, I looked around. "It sure is a nice day," I said.

The girl looked up and around. "It sure is," she said. "There's not a single cloud in the sky, and it looks like it's going to be—"

She abruptly halted her sentence. Not only that, but her jaw fell, and her eyes widened. She dropped the jug of water that she had been filling and pointed into the sky, her face filled with fear and alarm.

"Look at that!" she shouted. *"What in the world is that?!?!"*

I turned and looked up. Immediately, I, too, felt the fear and alarm that the girl was already experiencing.

Something was moving in the sky. It wasn't a plane, as it was round and silvery. And it wasn't a meteorite, as it was moving too slowly. It was moving erratically across the sky, trailing a brown line of smoke, and I was struck with the idea that, although it was a craft of some sort, it most obviously was in trouble and was going to crash.

The girl spoke.

"What is *that?*" she asked again.

"It looks like a flying saucer," I said, surprised to hear those words come out of my mouth. While I'd read all about flying saucers and UFOs, I'd never seen one before. For that fact, I never really believed they existed. I knew the universe was big, and I kind of figured that there probably would be life on other planets, but most of the stories and pictures that I had read or seen were made up from somebody's wild imagination.

Moments later, the flying saucer—or whatever it was—vanished beneath the trees. We stood staring and listening, but we saw nothing more, and we didn't hear an explosion or anything out of the ordinary.

"Do you think it crashed?" the girl asked.

"I think so," I said. "That was really crazy."

"Let's go look for it," the girl said. "I've never seen a flying saucer before."

"I don't think flying saucers exist," I said.

"Then, what do you think it was?" the girl replied. "It sure looked like a flying saucer to me."

She had a point. I got a good enough look at the craft to know that it wasn't a plane. It wasn't a balloon, and it certainly wasn't a helicopter. It really did look just like a flying saucer from a science fiction movie.

"I'm not sure what it was," I said, "but I'll go look for it with you."

"I'm Amber Duncan," the girl said as she knelt down and picked up the jug of water she'd dropped. Much of the water had spilled out, and she refilled it beneath the spigot.

"I'm Damon Lewis," I said. "My family is from Boston."

"I'm from Hartford, Connecticut," said Amber. "My family vacations here every year." She finished filling her water jug and stepped aside. I knelt down and began filling the plastic jug in my hand.

"This is our first time here," I said. "I figured we might see a lot of animals, but I never thought I'd see a flying saucer."

"Me, neither," Amber replied. Once again,

she looked up, searching the blue sky for any signs of something strange. By now, the smoke that had been trailing the doomed craft had faded away.

I pointed. "It looks like it went down about a mile away," I said. "Something that big shouldn't be too difficult to find."

"I wonder if anyone else saw it," Amber said. "We can't be the only ones."

"I'm sure there must be others," I said. "I wish I would've had my camera."

"I've got to take these water jugs back to our campsite," Amber said. "How about I meet you back here in an hour?"

"Sounds good," I said. "See you in an hour."

She walked away, and I finished filling the plastic water jug, excited to tell my family what I'd seen, anxious to find the crashed flying saucer or whatever it was. If I knew then what I know now, I certainly wouldn't have been so anxious, as I never knew that a simple hike could turn out to be so dangerous . . . and deadly.

"Mom! Dad!" I exclaimed as I returned to our campsite carrying the heavy water jugs. "Did you see it?"

My sister, Tracy, was sitting in a lawn chair by the smoldering fire. My voice caught her attention, and she turned.

"See what?" she asked.

Mom and Dad were standing just outside of their tent, sipping coffee. They looked at me expectantly, waiting for me to continue.

"A flying saucer!" I said as I put the water

jug on the ground near a large cooler. Then, I pointed off into the distance. "Over there!" I continued. "I was filling up the water jug, and I saw it in the sky. It looked like it was in trouble, because smoke was trailing behind. Then, it vanished beneath the trees."

My sister rolled her eyes. "Yeah, right," she said.

"I'm serious!" I said. "I saw it. So did Amber Duncan, a girl I met at the water spigot. She saw it, too. We're going to go look for it."

"We didn't see anything," Dad said, shaking his head. "But if you see any little green men, be sure to get their autograph. I'd like to have an autograph from a space alien."

"I'm not kidding!" I said. "I'm not sure exactly what we saw, but we saw *something*. It wasn't a plane, it wasn't a helicopter, and it certainly wasn't a balloon."

My sister rolled her eyes again, and now I saw that she had a book in her lap. She opened it and began reading.

I gave up trying to convince them that Amber and I had spotted something in the sky. After all: we didn't know exactly what we'd seen, anyway.

But I knew we saw something. Something had been traveling across the sky; something had crashed, I was certain, and not too far away.

And Amber and I were going to find it.

Time passed slowly. I wanted to begin our hike; I wanted to get searching right away.

Finally, nearly an hour had passed since Amber and I had departed from the water spigot. I hoped she had finished her chores and was ready.

"I'm going to go and look for that flying saucer," I announced.

Mom and Dad had been relaxing in lawn chairs, and my sister was still reading.

"Take a trail map with you," Dad said. "And don't go anywhere else. Stay on the trails and don't wander away from them."

Tracy dropped her book to the ground and stood. "I'm going to go with you," she said. "I want

29

to see this 'flying saucer.'"

"Don't forget my autograph," Dad said with a wink.

I must admit, I did feel a little silly. If someone told me they saw a flying saucer, that they thought it crashed nearby, I'm not sure if I would have believed them.

But I knew what I had seen. And my new friend, Amber, saw it, too. It was out there, somewhere. All we had to do was find it.

"And be sure to take your camera," Mom said. "Be sure to get some pictures."

It was obvious that they didn't believe me, but I didn't care. If we actually found the thing, if we actually came back with pictures, then they would have to believe me.

Amber and I zigzagged through the scattered campsites, making our way to the water spigot. Amber was already waiting.

"Hi, Amber," I said as we approached. "This is my sister, Tracy."

Amber and Tracy nodded to each other and

exchanged hellos.

"My brother says you and he saw a flying saucer," Tracy said.

Amber nodded. "Well," Amber replied, "we're not exactly sure *what* we saw. But it sure looked like a flying saucer, and we think we know where it crashed."

"Let's go," I said. "I can't wait to find it!"

"Even if we don't find anything," Amber said, "it will still be a fun adventure."

Amber's words would come back to haunt me, because what we were about to experience would, in no way, resemble a fun adventure. Deep down, I guess I never really expected to find the remains of a crashed alien spacecraft. It was fun to think about, but it just seemed too incredible to be true.

We probably won't find anything, I thought.

I was about to realize how wrong I was.

Soon, we had left the campsites behind. I had tucked the trail map in my back pocket, and I pulled it out, unfolding it as we walked.

"There are trails all over this place," I said.

Amber pointed. "I think we have to go that way," she said.

I stopped and inspected the map.

"There's a trail that goes off in that direction," I said, looking up and pointing. "Let's follow it and see if we find anything."

While we walked, we talked a bit more and

got to know each other. I liked Amber, and I could tell that Tracy did, too. She seemed like she was a lot like me.

"How come you're so sure that what you saw was a flying saucer?" Tracy asked.

"Well," Amber said, "we're not exactly sure what we saw. But it sure looked like a flying saucer, didn't it, Damon?"

I nodded. "That's what it looked like to me," I said.

"Yeah," Tracy said, "but you're *always* making up silly stories."

"I don't make up stories!" I insisted. "The only time I make up stories is when I'm writing them."

Which was true. I've always had a good imagination, and I like to write short stories about all sorts of things.

"Maybe you'll have a lot to write about after we find the flying saucer," Amber said.

We continued walking along the trail, peering through the forest, looking for anything out of the ordinary.

"We can't be far," Amber said as she stopped for a moment and placed her hands on her hips. Tracy and I stopped, too, and the three of us looked around.

The forest was really beautiful. We live in a subdivision in Boston, and we don't really have thick, wooded forests like what we were seeing. Oh, there are a few parks and other hiking areas not far from where we live, but not really anything like October Mountain State Forest.

"Hey," I said as I reached into my left front pocket and pulled out my digital camera that I had gotten for my birthday the year before. "I have an idea. Take our picture over by those trees and that big rock," I said, and I handed my camera to Tracy.

Amber and I walked to where the rock was. It was surrounded by a wall of small trees and thick branches choked with leaves. It would make a backdrop for a cool picture.

Amber and I turned around to face Tracy. We were both smiling . . . but not for long.

Amber's eyes suddenly flew wide open. She gasped and leapt back. Her arm shot out, and she pointed above my head.

"Damon!" she shouted. *"Look out! Run!"*

The sudden terror in Amber's voice was contagious, and I, too, was filled with horror without even knowing what the threat was. I leapt back and turned around, only to see a large, gray wasp's nest hanging from a branch. It had been just inches above my head. Because of the thick branches and the tightly knitted leaves, I hadn't seen it.

I took several more steps backward and noticed a few dark wasps buzzing around in the air circling and coiling toward the nest. One came so close that I could hear its wings buzzing past my ear.

"Whoa," I said as I took even more steps backward. "I'm glad I didn't bump into that."

"I got stung by two wasps last year," Amber said. "It hurt really bad."

"I stepped on a yellow jacket, and he bit my heel," Tracy said.

"Yellow jackets don't bite," I said. "They have stingers on their rear ends."

"Whatever," Tracy said with a shrug. "It hurt, and I screamed bloody murder."

"After being stung last year," Amber said, "I don't ever want to get stung again."

Tracy held up the camera.

"Say 'cheese,'" she said.

Amber and I stepped closer to one another, faced Tracy, and smiled. There was a faint, electronic chirping sound as my sister took the picture.

"Not bad," Tracy said. "Amber, you look okay, but Damon, you look scary."

I rolled my eyes and shook my head.

Sisters, I thought.

Tracy handed my camera back to me, and we started out again, following the trail as it wound through the lush forest. The only sound we could hear were birds in the trees.

"So, where is this flying saucer?" Tracy asked impatiently.

"I don't know," I replied. "And the forest is so thick, we might not even see it."

The trail turned sharply to the right, then to the left. Then, it angled up steeply, and my legs ached as we struggled to make it to the top of the hill. But we made it . . . and that's where our world was about to change.

We stood at the top of the hill, gazing down into a wide, open field. The three of us saw the object at the same time, and there was absolutely no mistake about it: what we were looking at was a real, honest-to-goodness flying saucer. It was silvery, disc-shaped, and very, very large, probably about the size of two semi-trucks put together and as tall as a two-story building. It had what appeared to be windows, but if that's what they were, they were covered with gray panels.

And now that we had proven to ourselves

that what we'd seen in the sky was actually a real flying saucer, we also proved something else: it had crashed. The craft was partially buried in the earth, and there was a large, jagged tear in the hull.

"I can't believe it," Tracy whispered. *"You were right, Damon. It's a real flying saucer."*

"Do you think there are space aliens on board?" Amber asked.

"There must be," I said. "I don't think flying saucers fly by themselves. They must have someone—or some *thing*—to pilot them."

"Let's go look!" Tracy said, and I was surprised by her sudden excitement and bravery. "Let's go see the space aliens!"

I, however, wasn't as enthusiastic as my sister. I really hadn't expected to find anything. Now that we had discovered the remains of a doomed spaceship, I wasn't so sure that it would be a good idea to go poking our noses around.

"Maybe it would be best to get Mom and Dad," I said.

"That would mean we would have to hike all the way back," Amber said. "I say we go and take a look. Besides: the space aliens were probably killed in the crash. Let's go check it out."

"All right," I agreed. But a little voice inside my mind continued to tell me that we were headed for trouble.

It was a voice I should have listened to.

We walked through the tall grass down the sharp slope, moving slowly and cautiously, but our gaze remained on the amazing site in the middle of the field.

"This is like something out of the movies," Amber said.

"Even better," I said. "This isn't a movie. This is *real*."

And there it was again: that tiny voice in my head, telling me to turn around, to go back, to leave the flying saucer in the field and head back to our campsite.

And once again, I pushed that little voice away.

I stopped at the bottom of the hill.

"Hang on a second," I said as I reached into my pocket and pulled out my camera. "I'm going to get a picture."

I turned the camera on and held it in front of me, finding the crashed flying saucer in the small, rectangular viewfinder. I took a couple of pictures, then returned it to my pocket.

"Cool," I said. "Let's go check it out."

It didn't take us long to reach the doomed spacecraft. Within minutes, we were standing only a few dozen feet from it, gazing at it in awe and wonder.

But now that we were so close to it, Amber and Tracy had become a little apprehensive. Before, they had been the ones who really wanted to get close to it. Now, they weren't so sure. I think they were a little afraid, just like I was.

"Maybe we shouldn't go any farther," Tracy

said. "It might be dangerous."

"I was thinking the same thing," Amber said. "We don't know what we're getting ourselves into. Maybe we should go and tell someone, like you suggested, Damon."

Now, it was my turn to be the brave one.

"Nonsense," I said. "You guys are just being scaredy-cats. We're already here. We might as well check it out."

And just to prove how brave I was, I began walking, hurrying toward the spacecraft, holding my camera in front of me, taking pictures as I got closer and closer. I walked right up to the flying saucer until I was standing near the gaping hole that had been torn open. The gash was about two feet wide, and it stretched from the bottom of the craft where it was buried in the earth all the way up to the top of it.

"Be careful," Tracy said. "You don't know what's in there."

Actually, I was every bit afraid as Amber and Tracy, but I wasn't going to let it show. I was going to show them that I was the brave one.

So, I took a step closer to the opening.

Closer.

Another step.

I tried to peer inside, through the shadowy, jagged gap in the side of the flying saucer, but all I could see was blackness.

Maybe Amber was right, I thought. *Maybe all of the space aliens were killed in the crash.*

But when I looked down, I saw something that was about to change everything.

Footprints.

They were strange and unlike any other tracks I'd ever seen. But there was no mistaking what I was looking at. They were definitely footprints in the soft earth, and they were most definitely not made by anything human.

"Amber! Tracy!" I shouted, pointing to the ground. "Come here! Check this out!"

Now that a few moments had passed, they realized that there probably wasn't any danger. Amber and Tracy hurried to my side as I knelt down to the ground, staring in amazement.

"Look at this!" I said. "These are footprints!"

Amber knelt beside me, followed by Tracy. The three of us inspected the strange tracks in the dirt. They were claw-like and very large, at least twice the size of our footprints. Maybe bigger. Whatever made them was probably quite large.

I looked around, peering across the field, expecting to see some strange, alien creature looking at us. I saw nothing, and I returned to inspecting the tracks at my feet.

Amber pointed, sweeping her finger above the ground, motioning her arm along the side of the massive flying saucer.

"Whatever it was," she said, "it looks like it went that way."

"And look at that," my sister said. She was pointing to a mysterious engraving on the side of the flying saucer. I hadn't seen it before, and I stood and walked toward it. Amber and Tracy followed.

It was a large circle, the size of a beach ball.

Strange squiggly lines—letters or words, I presumed—were scrawled beneath it, but it was a weird language I'd never seen before.

There was something very familiar about the circle, but I couldn't put my finger on it . . . at first. There were some lines that stretched across the circle and what appeared to be craters and mountains.

Suddenly, I realized what I was looking at.

"That's Mars!" I suddenly exclaimed. *"That's the Red Planet!"*

"How do you know?" Tracy asked. "It's not even red. It's just an engraving in the metal."

"I would know those features anywhere," I said. "Do you remember when I did my science report about Mars?"

Tracy shook her head. "No," she said.

"Well, I did. Last year. I studied all sorts of pictures and diagrams about Mars, and I'm telling you, that engraving is Mars."

"But I didn't think there was life on Mars," Amber said. "At least, none of the unmanned Mars explorations have found anything."

"Yeah," I agreed, "but there's a lot we don't know about the planet. The unmanned explorations haven't covered much territory. Even scientists agree that there is a possibility that there's life on Mars, and this flying saucer proves it!"

We were silent for a moment, trying to take in the weight of our discovery.

Martians, I thought. *Science fiction has now become science fact. There is life on Mars! Martians really do exist!*

Tracy looked at the ground. "But where did they go?" she asked. "If they're still alive, where are they?"

"Good question," I replied. "But they can't be far."

"Let's follow the tracks," Amber suggested.

Tracy shook her head. "Not me," she said. "We have no idea what those things might do to us. I heard that Martians and space aliens kidnap people and perform horrible experiments on them in their spaceships."

I rolled my eyes. "Oh, please," I sneered. "That's just in the movies and in books."

Tracy shook her head. "No, it's not," she said. "I saw it on TV a few weeks ago. A man and his wife said they were abducted by aliens, and the creatures performed awful experiments on them."

"And you believe that?" I asked.

"I saw it on TV," Tracy repeated.

Amber spoke up. "Just because you saw it on TV doesn't mean it's true, no matter who says it. People make up stuff like that all the time and tell people that it's real. I say we follow the tracks and look for the Martian."

"Let's do it," I said. "We'll keep our eyes out and be careful."

"I'll go with you," Tracy said, "but only because I don't want to be left alone. But I'm telling you: if I get abducted by Martians, you're going to be in big trouble."

"If we get abducted by Martians," I said, "we're *all* going to be in trouble."

Later, after we'd been captured and taken to the flying saucer by the horrible Martians, I'd wished we'd listened to my sister.

But by then, it was too late.

Following the tracks was easy, because they were clearly defined in the soft earth. I figured that whatever had made them—Martians—were probably quite large and heavy.

It was also very apparent that there was probably more than one, as we seemed to be following not one set of tracks, but several.

"Maybe they're friendly," Amber said. "Maybe they just want to go home."

"Maybe they're hurt," Tracy said. "Maybe they need to go to the hospital."

That almost sounded funny, and I tried to imagine the looks on the faces of the doctors and nurses at the hospital when aliens from another planet arrived seeking help. They would cause chaos and panic! Everyone would be screaming and running for the doors.

We followed the strange tracks through the field and into the forest. I was mindful about what my dad had told me, about not leaving the trail. But I also knew that we really wouldn't get lost, because we could always follow the tracks back to the flying saucer.

At the edge of the forest, we stopped. The tracks continued on through the woods.

"I don't see anything," Amber said as she looked around.

"Well," I said, "it's been a couple of hours since we saw the flying saucer in the sky. They can't be too far, but they still have had enough time to travel a good distance."

"Maybe they're hiding," Tracy said. "Maybe they're scared."

"Maybe," I said. "We won't know until we see them."

"Let's keep going," Amber said. "Let's follow the tracks into the woods. Move slow, and keep your eyes open."

And it wasn't long before we found exactly what we were looking for.

I spotted it first. I saw some branches moving unnaturally, and it was very obvious that the wind hadn't disturbed them.

"Stop!" I hissed, grabbing Tracy and Amber by the shoulders. Then, I pointed. *"Up there!"* I said. *"Up by that clump of spruce trees!"*

While Amber and Tracy looked where I was pointing, I suddenly realized that the three of us were out in the open, in full view. It might be best to not show ourselves.

I snapped my head around, looking for somewhere to hide. Thankfully, there was a large boulder about twenty feet to the right of us.

"Quick!" I said. "Let's get behind that rock! We need to get out of sight!"

The three of us ran behind the boulder and huddled together, peering around the large rock. We could still see the branches shaking and moving, and we waited for something to appear.

I'm going to feel really silly if it's just a deer, I thought.

I needn't have worried about feeling silly, because what suddenly appeared wasn't a deer. It wasn't a bear, it wasn't another human.

It was something altogether different, something no one on Earth had ever seen before.

Amber, Tracy, and I were the first human beings to ever see a real, live Martian.

Tracy opened her mouth and gasped, and I knew she was about to scream. However, before she could, I quickly placed my hand over her mouth.

"Shhhh!" I whispered. *"If you scream, he's going to see us."*

The Martian emerged from the branches and was now in full view. He was the most incredible creature I had ever seen. I was both fascinated and horrified, as it was exciting to know that we were being visited by Martians. Still, we had no idea whether he was friendly, and we couldn't take our chances. So, the three of us just hunkered behind the boulder and watched.

He was tall, just as I had suspected. Probably a couple of feet taller than my dad, but his body was human-like, with two arms and two legs. I remember seeing a science fiction movie about invading space aliens that had three heads and six arms, but the creature we were seeing didn't look anything like that.

The thing that was most noticeable was his head, which was twice the size of what a human's head would be. He was wearing a tight-fitting suit, and only his hands and head were exposed, showing smooth, green skin.

I suddenly remembered my camera, and I carefully pulled it from my pocket, found the Martian in the viewfinder, and took a couple of pictures. I tried to zoom in, but the pictures turned out blurry. But then I switched it over into movie mode and recorded a short clip.

"What's wrong with him?" Amber asked. "He's acting kind of strange."

Which was an odd thing to say, being that we knew nothing about the alien. He might have been acting completely normal for a Martian.

But I understood what Amber meant. The Martian really did appear confused and disoriented, like he didn't know what he was doing or where he was.

"Maybe he was hurt in the crash," Tracy said. "Maybe he bumped his head, and it made him dizzy."

That was possible, too. Anything was possible. He was a being from another planet, and we knew nothing of his behaviors . . . or what he was capable of.

But we were about to find out. I thought we were hidden behind the boulder, but somehow, the Martian spotted us.

How did I know this?

He stopped moving, looked in our direction, and started running toward us.

There was only one thing we could do, and the three of us did it at the same time.

We ran.

We ran as fast as we could, each of us taking off in different directions. Tracy was screaming, Amber was screaming, and I might've been screaming, too. I was so terrified, I don't remember. All I remember is that I wanted to get away from that thing as fast as I could. I remember wondering how fast the Martian could move, and what he would do if he caught one of us.

Maybe Tracy is right, I thought as I sprinted through the field. *Maybe space aliens do kidnap humans. Maybe they really do perform horrible experiments on their bodies.*

I didn't want to find out. I just wanted to get away alive.

I turned and looked over my shoulder to see where the Martian was, surprised to see him stopped in the field. Once again, he looked confused and disoriented. He was still watching us, glancing back and forth between Tracy, Amber, and me. It was as if he knew he couldn't capture all three of us and was trying to pick one victim.

Unfortunately, that victim was *me.*

With amazing speed, he came at me. Then, it was *my* turn to scream, and I shouted as loud as I possibly could as I raced across the field. I had no idea where to go, really. I didn't want to go anywhere near the crashed spacecraft that was looming in the distance. And I wasn't sure if I could actually make it to the trail. I certainly didn't have time to stop and consult the map in my back pocket.

So, I just ran and ran and ran. I ran as if my life depended on it. As a matter of fact, my life *did* depend on it. I didn't even look back over my shoulder, because I didn't want to risk misstepping, tripping, and falling. Then, it would be too late, as I knew the Martian would easily overtake me.

But one thing I didn't know . . .

It was already too late.

The Martian was impossibly fast, faster than a deer or a gazelle. Probably faster than a cheetah.

I was suddenly sent sprawling forward, like I'd been hit by a truck. I was hurled up into the air and completed two somersaults before slamming into the soft earth face-first. Horrified, I rolled to my back, intent on standing up and continuing my escape.

But that wasn't going to happen. Looming above me was the Martian. I heard Tracy or Amber screaming as the Martian suddenly lunged down upon me. The last thing I remember was the realization that it hadn't been Tracy or Amber screaming; it had been me, and my screams were silenced when the horrible Martian landed upon me, pinning me to the ground, trapping me beneath his enormous body.

Then, someone else was screaming. I knew it wasn't me, as I was so squished by the enormous space alien that I couldn't open my mouth. Even if I had been able to do that, the wind had been knocked out of me. I had screamed when the Martian fell upon me, but there was no way I would be able to scream as long as he was on top of me, as it was impossible to even take a breath.

I recognized Tracy's high-pitched scream. She'd obviously seen the Martian attack me, and she was just as horrified as I was.

But her screams distracted the Martian, and he rolled to his side to see who or what was making such a shrill sound.

That was the lucky break I needed. Despite the fact that I was gasping for air, I managed to scramble away, leap to my feet, and start running again. I knew I might not get very far, but I wasn't going to stay where I was, at the mercy of the horrible space alien. More and more, I had been thinking Tracy was right, after all: maybe Martians *did* abduct humans, and maybe they did take them back to their spaceships where they performed horrible experiments on their bodies. That would be awful.

Running was difficult, but gradually, I was able to catch my breath and breathe easier. Tracy had stopped screaming. She had met up with Amber, and they were racing in my direction. The Martian, however, wasn't pursuing us anymore. He got to his feet and looked around curiously, as if he was confused.

The terrible thing is that he's so unpredictable,

I thought. *It's impossible to tell what he's going to do next.*

I stopped to see where Tracy and Amber were. They had almost reached me, and I pointed into the distance, the top of the hill where we'd first spotted the crashed alien spacecraft. In the field, the Martian was still holding his ground, looking just as confused and disoriented as ever.

"We've got to try to make it back to our campsite!" I said as the girls reached me. I started running again, and the three of us flew through the tall grass, racing as fast as we could. We reached the trail and scrambled up the hill. At the top, we paused to catch our breaths and to see if the Martian was chasing us.

"Look at him," Amber said. "Why is he acting like that?"

The Martian remained in the field where he'd tackled me. Now, however, his body was convulsing and shaking. He made a couple of leaps into the air and then began spinning in circles.

"It's like he's gone crazy or something," I

said.

"Maybe that's just how Martians are," my sister said.

Tracy had a good point. We knew nothing about the Martian, and for all we knew, this could be his normal behavior.

"Let's just get out of here while we have a chance," Amber said. "We need to report this to the police."

"Yeah," Tracy said. "They need to come out here and arrest him."

The thought was almost funny. In my mind, I saw a couple of police officers leading the Martian away in handcuffs. I almost laughed out loud.

We raced down the hill and continued along the trail, glad to be away from the horrifying space alien, thankful we'd been able to escape. By now I was certain that we would make it back to camp, that our ordeal was over.

But I had made an assumption without thinking. For some reason, I never considered that there might be more than one Martian. It would only make sense that there might be three, four, five, or maybe ten or more space aliens traveling in the flying saucer. I don't know why, but at the time, the thought never occurred to me that there would possibly be more Martians.

But when we saw what was waiting for us on the other side of a small hill, I realized that there was a good chance that not only would we *not* make it back to our campsite . . . we might not make it out of October Mountain State Forest alive.

Amber saw them first, and she stopped running so abruptly that I ran into her, knocking her to the ground. It was only after I was helping her up that I saw what had caused her to halt. Tracy, too, saw what was ahead of us on the trail. She screamed and stopped so suddenly that her shoes left gouges in the trail.

Ahead of us were four Martians. They looked identical to the one that had attacked us in the field.

And just like the Martian in the field, the

four space aliens up ahead seemed confused. They were moving toward us, but their bodies were making quirky, jerky motions. Again, I wondered if it was just a Martian characteristic or if there was something wrong with them, if they had all been injured in the crash.

"Now what?" Amber said in a voice just above a whisper.

"Back up really slow," I said. "We'll go back the way we came and see if we can hide in the woods."

"But what about that other ugly Martian in the field?" Tracy asked. "What if he's coming after us?"

I turned and looked behind us.

"I don't see him," I said. "Besides: we don't have any other choice. Start backing up slowly. Maybe, if they don't think of us as a threat, they'll leave us alone. That'll give us time to hide."

The three of us began backing up slowly. Our eyes never left the Martians that, thankfully, remained on the trail in front of us, showing no

74

signs of pursuit. When we reached the other side of the small hill, we turned and began running. All the while, I looked deep in the woods, to the left and to the right, for a place to hide. Finally, I spotted a thick stand of spruce trees. They were tightly knitted together, and their branches hung low to the ground. If we could make it to those trees undetected, we could crawl beneath the branches and be hidden, should the Martians come after us.

"That way!" I said, pointing as I darted off the trail and into the woods. Amber and Tracy followed close behind, and the three of us crashed through brush and branches like deer.

"Where are we going?" Tracy asked.

"To those trees up there," I said. "We can hide beneath the branches, if we can get there without those things seeing us."

When we reached the stand of spruce trees, we stopped running. I turned around to look for the Martians. There was no sign of them.

I grabbed a few of the low hanging branches

and pulled them to the side, ignoring the needles that poked my skin.

"Get down!" I ordered Amber and Tracy. "Crawl under the branches and keep low!"

After my sister and Amber had crawled beneath the branches, it was my turn. The needles continued to poke my exposed skin, but I hardly noticed them. Within seconds, the three of us were nestled on the ground beneath the canopy of spruce branches.

"Do you think we're hidden enough?" Amber asked.

She had just spoken those words when we caught movement on the distant trail. Peering through the thick, spiny branches, we could make out the enormous Martians on the trail. They were moving fast, as if on a mission.

Amber's question hung in my mind.

Do you think we're hidden enough?

We were about to find out.

The three of us held our breaths, and it occurred to me that if the Martians did find us, we'd be done for. There was nowhere we could go. Our only hope was to sit tight, stay where we were, remain quiet, and hope that the Martians passed us by.

We weren't going to be so lucky.

On the trail, the group of Martians suddenly stopped. As if they had picked up our scent, they turned and looked in our direction. Once again, their movements were jerky and quick. I didn't know if they could see us, but I had an awful, sinking suspicion that they knew we were close by.

One by one, the Martians left the trail and entered the woods, coming toward us. Beside me, my sister grabbed my hand and squeezed. She was terrified, and I was, too. Sure, I'm her older brother, and I'm supposed to protect her and be brave.

But, then again, I'd never been faced with gigantic aliens from another planet. I was just as terrified as she was.

"Now what do we do?" Amber whispered, and her voice trembled.

"The only thing we can do," I replied quietly. "If we move, they'll see us for sure. Maybe if we stay where we are and don't move, they won't know where we are."

Without any other option, we sat tight. I felt completely helpless, and I wondered if I'd made the right decision, after all. Maybe we should have continued on the trail until we found a better place to hide.

But, then again, I thought, *we would still*

have that other Martian to worry about.

Branches broke and twigs snapped as the hulking Martians made their way through the forest, moving closer to us with every step. Tracy's grip on my hand was nearly crushing my bones. Amber had grabbed my other hand, and she, too, was squeezing tightly.

Finally, the Martians stopped about ten feet in front of us. Very slowly, I leaned my head toward Amber until my lips were near her ear.

"I don't think they can see us," I whispered.

The Martians' movements were more agitated, more jerky than ever. It appeared as if they were looking for us, as if they could actually smell us, but couldn't make us out behind the thick veil of spruce needles.

Then, one of the Martians took a step forward. In his right hand, he carried a strange gun, pistol-shaped, with what appeared to be several saucers around the barrel. Slowly, he raised it up, pointing it right at our hiding place. He made a hideous sound, a growl of gibberish that made no sense, a language that sounded nothing like any other language I'd heard.

Of course, that would be expected, when you're dealing with aliens from another planet!

A chill went through my body as I realized we'd been caught. Now, we were at the mercy of the Martian with the strange gun. We'd been found out, and I knew it. There was no choice but to surrender, as there was no telling what he would do with the gun.

I pulled my hands away from Tracy and Amber and slowly crawled out from beneath the spruce branches. I raised both of my hands in the air. Behind me, Amber and Tracy did the same.

They looked at us.

We looked at them.

The Martian carrying the gun raised it higher and pointed directly at me. Then, he pulled the trigger . . . .

There was a loud clicking sound when the Martian pulled the trigger. All three of us trembled violently.

I wasn't sure what I had expected, but I was certainly surprised to suddenly find myself immobilized, wrapped tightly in some sort of strange, plastic wrap. The gun wasn't a gun, after all, but some sort of spraying device. In an instant, I was frozen, a prisoner of some strange, tightly wrapped material. The entire process took less than a second, and the Martian quickly repeated the process on Tracy and Amber.

From my neck all the way to my feet, I was covered and completely wrapped, a human ham sandwich. The feeling was terrifying. I couldn't move my legs, I couldn't move my arms. The only thing I could move was my head. I could move my lips, I could talk, I could breathe. I could hear and smell.

But I couldn't walk. I couldn't use my arms to defend myself.

Tracy shrieked when she found out she couldn't move. Amber struggled and tried to get out of the plastic covering that had already enshrouded her body, but it was too late. She, too, was quickly immobilized, frozen.

My heart was racing and my mind was frantic. Without the ability to run and flee, without the ability to escape, we were powerless against the Martians that towered over us.

One of the other Martians approached me and easily picked me up with one claw-like hand and threw me over his shoulder. Yet another

Martian picked up both Amber and Tracy, and then the group began to move. They carried us back to the trail, across the field, and to the crashed flying saucer. One of the Martians approached the spacecraft and waved his hand in front of one of the panels. Instantly, the panel slid up, creating a doorway, an entry to and from the saucer. The Martian strode inside where lights suddenly illuminated the interior of the craft.

Then, the Martian that was carrying me stepped into the spacecraft.

I looked around. Oddly enough, what I was seeing appeared to be very similar to what I'd seen in most science fiction movies. The inside of the flying saucer contained what appeared to be computer screens, flashing lights on glowing panels, large seats big enough to fit the Martians, and what was most obviously a cockpit designed for the pilot or captain of the craft.

But it was something else that I noticed, something else that appeared familiar, that made me cringe in horror.

Near the far wall was a series of beds with strong straps attached to them, made to hold down a victim, to prevent them from escaping.

It was then that I realized that everything I'd heard about alien abductions was true. Everything people had said about being taken aboard flying saucers, of having horrible experiments performed on their bodies was true. They were not making it up. It actually happened.

And now, it was going to happen again.

To us.

The Martian lowered me to the floor, onto my back. The feeling of being utterly powerless was terrifying, and knowing that I was going to be used for bizarre alien experiments was even more horrifying. My heart beat faster than ever, and my breaths were shallow and quick.

Amber and Tracy were laid down next to me.

"What's . . . what's going to happen to us?" Tracy stammered.

"Nothing," I lied. Apparently, Tracy hadn't

seen the beds with the straps, and I wasn't going to tell her about them. That would only make her even more scared than she already was.

I tried moving my hands and found that I could wiggle my fingers a tiny bit. It took a lot of work, but the more I kept at it, the more I could move them around. Still, the feeling of helplessness was overwhelming, but I continued wiggling my fingers just to be able to move some part of my body, to convince my mind that maybe, somehow, there was a way out of this.

I looked around. The strange aliens were busy doing other things, almost as if they had forgotten about us. They were talking in weird, alien gibberish, and I wondered if they were talking about what experiments they were going to perform on us.

"Maybe someone will come looking for us," Amber said, trying to sound hopeful. "If we're gone too long, my parents are going to try to find us. Maybe we'll be saved."

It was a nice thought, but I didn't think it

was very likely. Still, I wasn't going to say anything and destroy her hope. Right now, hope was all we had.

Meanwhile, I had succeeded in not only being able to wiggle my fingers, but move my hand around. It had been pressed against my thigh, over my right pocket, and I could feel the hard lump of my pocket knife beneath my palm.

If I can only move my hand enough to get my knife, I thought. *If I can get my hand into my pocket and somehow open the blade, maybe I can cut some of this stuff away from me.*

Sure, I didn't know how I would be able to do it with the Martians around. I was certain they would see what I was up to and probably spray more of that gunk on me until they were ready to perform their horrible experiments.

The Martians continued their busy work around the flying saucer, and I wondered if they were trying to make repairs. I had no idea how they would fix the enormous crack in the hull, and I figured that the craft was useless until they fixed it. Still, other functions of the spaceship seemed to perform properly. Several times I heard what sounded like engines starting, only to hear them come to an abrupt, choking halt. When this happened, the Martians grunted and snarled in their native alien gibberish.

And I kept working my fingers and my hand. Finally, I was able to move my hand enough to pull it back and shove my fingers into my pocket. When my palm touched my knife, it was such a feeling of triumph and glory that I felt like shouting.

But I knew I still had a lot of work to do. I still had to get the blade open, and I still hadn't figured out how I would try to cut the plastic-type material away from me without the Martians knowing what I was up to.

Suddenly, I heard a sound that was instantly familiar: the squawking of a crow. It was very loud, as if it had perched in a tree not far from the crashed flying saucer.

The crow's squawks drew the immediate attention of the Martians. Curious, they hurried to the door and hustled outside.

It was the chance I needed. It was difficult, but I managed to use a couple of my fingers to open the blade of my pocket knife. I held the handle and pressed the sharp end into the plastic material covering me. The blade pierced the rubbery fabric, and to my surprise, as I drew the blade in an upward motion, I encountered little difficulty in slicing through the material.

Amber saw what I was doing.

"Hurry, Damon!" she hissed. "Hurry and free yourself! Then, you can free Tracy and me!"

I worked frantically, every so often glancing out the open door to see if the Martians were coming back. Apparently, they were intensely curious about what was making the noise. I hoped they were curious enough to give me time to get free.

That's all I needed: time.

Would there be enough? I wasn't sure, but I had to try. I had to hope.

I kept working . . . .

As the seconds ticked past, I worked faster and faster. The more I did, the more the strange, plastic wrappings peeled away as my blade slid through.

Finally, I was free, and I scrambled to my feet. On the floor, the plastic sheeting that had covered me looked like a torn plastic bag, like a snake had shed its skin.

Tracy was right next to me, so I started with her. Beginning at her feet, I carefully placed the blade against the material and cautiously drew the knife upward, not wanting to cut her clothing or skin. Freeing Tracy was much easier than freeing myself, and in seconds, my sister was on her feet, and I was working to cut the material away from Amber.

It seemed impossible, but the three of us were now standing in the spacecraft, alone, able to walk, able to move our fingers, hands, and arms.

But we certainly weren't out of danger.

I folded my knife and returned it to my front pocket. Then, I placed my index finger to my lips.

"Stay here!" I hissed, and I tiptoed to the spacecraft's open entryway. Peering outside, I saw no sign of the Martians. Perhaps they decided that crow was an enemy, and they were going to try to chase it down. I didn't know, and I didn't care. All I knew was that now we had a fighting chance. Now, we could escape. All we had to do was slip away without the Martians seeing us.

I motioned for Tracy and Amber to come by me, and that's when I noticed something I hadn't seen before. In a rack on the wall next to me were half a dozen rifles of some sort. They were big, probably twice as big as a normal rifle used by humans. But I was sure they were some sort of gun, maybe even one of those strange goo-guns the Martians had used on us.

I reached for one and pulled it from the rack, surprised at how light it was in relation to its size.

"What's that?" Tracy asked.

"It's got to be a gun of some sort," I replied. "Grab one. You, too, Amber. We'll figure out how to use them when the time comes."

Amber and Tracy each pulled a gun from the rack. I imagine we looked pretty silly standing there in the doorway of a flying saucer, three kids carrying three large rifles.

But there was no time to worry about how silly we looked. We had to slip away, and we had to do so quickly and quietly, without the Martians seeing us, wherever they were.

"Follow me," I said, and I slipped silently through the doorway.

The warm sunshine on my face gave me new life, new hope. We already had one victory: we'd escaped from the plastic wrap that had ensnared us. That alone was a nearly impossible feat, but we'd pulled it off.

I tried to imagine where the Martians might have gone, as there were only a few trees scattered in the field and the hilly forest in the distance. I was sure the Martians hadn't traveled across the field in such a short time, so I figured they were probably still close by, probably on the other side of the flying saucer.

So, I headed straight across the field, jogging through the grass, carrying the weapon over my shoulder. Tracy and Amber followed. Once in a while, I turned to glance over my shoulder to see if the Martians had spotted us. I saw no sign of them, and we didn't stop until we reached the forest. Then, and only then, after we'd found some thick brush to hide in, did we stop to catch our breaths and rest.

"We made it!" Amber said triumphantly.

"We got away!"

"We're not home yet," I said. "We still have to make it back to our campsites."

"Yeah," Tracy said, "but we got out of there. I have never been so scared in my life."

"Me, too," I admitted. "But let's not think about that now. Let's think about getting back to the campsite without being spotted."

I was feeling pretty good. We'd escaped from the Martians, and we'd put some good distance between us and the crashed flying saucer. We even had three of their guns that we'd stolen from the inside of the spacecraft. And it was a good thing, too . . . because we were going to need them.

We remained hidden in the bushes for a few minutes, resting and taking it easy, keeping an eye on the flying saucer in the distance, watching for the return of the Martians. I knew they couldn't be far away, and it was only a matter of time before they returned and discovered us missing.

I stood and pulled the trail map from my back pocket, unfolded it, and tried to get a bearing on where we were.

"Our campsite is over here," I said as I tapped the map with my finger. "Here's the trail we started out on, and here's the field. The quickest way to get back to the trail is by going across the field."

"But if we do that," Amber said, "we'll be in plain sight. The Martians will see us for sure."

"Exactly," I agreed. "That's why I think our best bet will be to stay out of the field and head through the woods. There's no trail to follow, but if we continue in a straight line for about a half mile, we'll run right into the hiking path. If we can make it that far, we're home free."

"I'm all for that," Amber said.

Tracy nodded. "Me, too," she said. "I want to go home. I'm tired, and I'm hungry."

I hadn't thought about it, but now that Tracy brought it up, I was hungry, too. I couldn't wait to get back to our campsite and explain to Mom and Dad what had happened while eating a huge peanut butter and jelly sandwich or maybe even a hamburger or hot dog.

"Let's get going," I said.

Amber and Tracy stood, and we began

hiking through the forest. Once again, I remembered what dad had told me, about not leaving the trail. Normally, I would've listened to him. But in this instance, we had no other choice. Besides: I really wasn't worried about getting lost. In looking at the map, there were any number of trails that we would run into if we just kept walking. Sure, October Mountain State Forest is an enormous park, and there were places where it would be really easy to get lost. But in the area where we were, many trails crisscrossed the terrain, and I wasn't worried about getting lost.

In fact, I was more worried about those Martians finding out that we had escaped and having them come after us. I was so worried about those Martians that I entirely forgot about the other Martian that we'd spotted earlier, the one that chased me across the field and knocked me to the ground.

That's the Martian I should have been worried about . . . because we were about to encounter him once again.

I didn't have a compass, so I used the sun and the angle of the shadows created by the trees to try and chart a straight course through the forest.

"I hope you know where you're going," my sister said.

"Don't worry," I said as I ducked beneath a branch. "We're not going to get lost."

While we walked, I was careful to look for any signs of the Martians. I was certain that, when they returned to their spacecraft and found us missing, they would be mad. They were probably really looking forward to performing their horrible experiments on us, and now that we had escaped and spoiled their fun, they were probably as mad as hornets.

Too bad for them, I thought smugly. *They're just going to have to experiment on somebody else.*

Walking was tough. Being that we weren't on any sort of trail or footpath, we had to blaze our own way, which meant pushing small saplings and branches out of our way. I know that doesn't sound like it would be too difficult, but after a while, it gets tiring. I began to wonder what early explorers did, men like Lewis and Clark who traveled hundreds and hundreds of miles through forests where no roads or trails existed.

So, you can imagine my relief when we suddenly came upon the trail. Instantly, I recognized it as the main trail, the path we had started out on.

"We made it!" Amber exclaimed. "Great job leading us through the woods, Damon!"

I smiled and felt a little proud. Getting

through the woods wasn't really all that big of a deal, but it was one more hurdle, one more obstacle we'd completed on our ultimate journey to make it back to our campsite.

Then, Tracy screamed . . . and that changed everything.

At the same time that Tracy screamed, her arm shot out with her index finger extended, pointing.

"There's one of them!" she shouted.

I spun and instinctively raised the long gun to my shoulder. On the trail ahead of us was a Martian. I could only assume that it was the Martian that had chased me down earlier. He had been walking in the other direction and might not have even spotted us, except for the fact that my sister screamed, causing him to turn and face us. He watched us curiously, making jerky movements and twitches. However, his motions were much faster, much more expressive than they had been earlier, and I wondered if he was sick or if there was something wrong with him.

"He's acting like a maniac," Amber whispered. *"It's like he's getting crazier and crazier. He's acting even weirder than he was when he chased us across the field."*

"Great," Tracy said. "Not only is he a Martian, but he's a maniac. A maniac Martian in Massachusetts. That's just what we need to make our day."

"Maybe he *is* getting crazier," I said, still leveling the gun at the enormous alien. "And that might make it much worse for us. Maniacs do things without thinking. If he's not in control of himself, there's no telling what he might do."

"At least he's not coming after us," Amber said. "We know how fast he can run, and I don't want to go through that again."

I was still holding the big gun to my shoulder. Honestly, I really knew nothing about

106

firearms. The only experience I've had with a weapon was a BB gun that I learned to shoot at my uncle's farmhouse in New Hampshire. Other than that, I'd never shot any other gun in my life.

But I was about to learn, whether or not I liked it.

As much as I'd hoped the maniac Martian wouldn't come after us, that hope was dashed when he suddenly began charging in our direction.

"*Shoot him!*" Amber shouted.

"*Yeah, Damon!*" my sister echoed. "*Shoot him! Shoot him!*"

I pulled the trigger, but it wouldn't move. No matter how hard I squeezed it, it wouldn't budge, not even the tiniest bit.

"Hurry!" Amber urged. "He's moving fast!"

"I can see that!" I snapped. "I just can't

figure out how to work this thing."

Amber raised the gun she was carrying and placed it to her shoulder. She, too, tried firing it, but encountered the same problem I did: the trigger wouldn't budge. The same thing happened with my sister. All three of us were trying to get the weapons to fire, but it was no use.

Meanwhile, the Martian was charging just as fast as ever, and the distance between him and us was getting smaller and smaller by the second. The space alien was acting even more crazy, flailing his arms about like a madman. He wasn't even running in a straight line, but zigzagging to the left and to the right.

"Run!" I shouted.

Lowering the guns, we spun and ran the opposite way on the trail, swinging the weapons at our sides. I thought about dropping the gun altogether, being that it was of no use to us, but I thought I'd keep it, just to be safe. I might be able to use it, or if I had another chance, maybe I could figure out how to fire it.

We ran as fast as we could for about a minute. My lungs were on fire, and my legs ached. I wasn't sure how long I could keep up the pace, and I knew that Amber and Tracy were struggling, too. We'd already exerted an enormous amount of energy over the course of the day, and it wouldn't be long before we were exhausted.

And the crazed, maniacal Martian was still coming after us. He showed no signs of tiring, no signs of slowing down.

Amber had finally had enough, but I was totally unexpected for what she was about to do.

"I can't keep going," she said. She stopped running and threw the gun to the ground.

I stopped and turned around.

"You've got to keep going!" I shouted. I pointed to the trail, to the Martian that was no more than fifty feet behind us, still charging as fast as ever in our direction.

"I can't!" Amber shouted. "I'm exhausted, and I'm mad! I hate that thing!"

With that, Amber did something I couldn't

believe: she began charging the Martian.

"Amber!" I cried. "Wait! What are you doing?!?! Come back! He'll tear you to shreds!"

By now, Tracy had stopped on the trail, and she, too, urged Amber to turn back around.

"Amber!" she shouted. "Don't! Come back!"

It was a sad realization when I figured out what Amber was doing. She had given up. She knew that there was no way she was going to escape from the Martian, so she decided to end it all right then and there by running straight into the arms of the crazed space alien!

"I can't watch!" Tracy said, and she covered her face with her hands.

I shouted one more time.

"Amber! Please! Don't do this!"

Amber paid no attention to me. Instead, she continued running toward the Martian . . . but then she did something even stranger. She began flailing her arms, zigzagging back and forth, even jumping off the ground, bouncing up and down. She shouted nonsensical things and behaved like a madwoman.

Hearing Amber's bizarre shouts, Tracy's hands fell from her face. She and I watched as the Martian stopped dead in his tracks. He was completely motionless.

Still, Amber continued her frantic, erratic motions as she ran toward the hulking space alien standing in the trail.

Then, something unbelievable happened.

The Martian spun and began running the other way!

All the while, Amber pressed on, charging after the Martian, even though he was retreating! She had gone totally, stark raving mad!

While we watched, the Martian vanished over a small hill, and Amber stopped in the middle of the trail. She put her hands on her hips and stared in the direction where the Martian had vanished. Then, she turned slowly, looked at Amber and me, and began walking back.

She smiled as she approached.

"I don't know what you did," I said, "but it worked."

Amber smiled and shrugged.

"I saw something like that on television," she replied. "It was an old movie where a man was surrounded by savages. He began jumping up and down and acting like a crazy person, and the savages became frightened. His behavior caused them to run away in terror. I wondered if the Martian would do the same thing."

"He could've killed you," Tracy said.

Again, Amber shrugged. "He probably would have, anyway," she said. "We couldn't get our guns to fire, so I figured anything was better than nothing. It was a gamble, for sure, but it worked."

I stared at Amber in disbelief. I don't think I'd ever met a braver person in my entire life.

"I thought he was going to tear you limb from limb," Tracy said. "I couldn't believe it when you started—"

"Shhh!" I said, placing my index finger to my lips. *"Listen!"*

We were silent for a moment. All we could hear were a few birds chirping in the trees and a slight wind that ruffled leaves and branches.

Then:

An entirely different sound altogether.

A thumping sound.

It was very faint at first and sounded like a heartbeat. Very quickly, however, the beats got faster and the sound grew louder. Soon, there was no mistaking what it was.

A helicopter.

Hope surged as the sound grew louder and louder.

Amber's arm shot out. "Right there! It's over there!"

Sure enough, there was a white helicopter cruising above the trees not far from where we were.

"I'll bet they saw the spaceship crash, and they're looking for it!" Tracy exclaimed. "Maybe they're even looking for us! We're going to be rescued! We're going to be safe!"

I tried to be as hopeful as Tracy; I tried to believe that this was all over, that our day of madness was about to come to an end.

Unfortunately, it was all just wishful thinking. Our ordeal wasn't finished. The Martians were a lot smarter than we thought, and they still had a few tricks up their sleeves . . . .

Unfortunately, the helicopter was too far away to see us, despite the fact that we jumped up and down and waved our arms. We were yelling and screaming, which was a bit silly when you think about it, because they would never have heard us. We were disappointed, but at least we knew that there were people around. Maybe they were looking for us, maybe they weren't. But seeing the helicopter sparked a new ray of hope in all of us.

"Let's keep going," Amber said.

I picked up my gun that was laying on the trail.

"First," I said, "I'm going to try to figure this thing out." Carefully, I inspected the trigger mechanism and the stock, and I quickly found the problem: just like most guns on Earth, there was a safety switch built in to keep the gun from firing accidentally.

"Hey, guys," I said. "I think I've figured these things out. Look here."

I showed Amber and Tracy the safety switch, demonstrating by clicking it on and off.

"I think they'll work now," I said. "If we need to use them again, be sure to switch the safety to the 'off' position. I don't know what will happen after that, but they are obviously weapons of some sort."

"Let's just hope we don't have to use them," Amber said.

"I'm hoping the same thing," Tracy said.

"But just think," I said, holding the rifle up as if it were a trophy. "What a great souvenir! Can you imagine taking this to school for show and tell?"

"You can't take a gun to school!" Amber said. "You'd be arrested!"

"Yeah," I said with a sigh. "You're probably right. But it would still look cool on my bedroom wall!"

"Mom and Dad won't let you keep that on your bedroom wall!" Tracy said.

"Yeah," I said. "You're right about that, too."

"I don't care about these guns," Amber said. "I just want to get out of here alive."

Once again, we started out along the hiking path. I knew we couldn't be more than twenty minutes away from the campsite, and I was really hoping that we wouldn't encounter that maniac Martian that had tried to chase us down.

And every time I thought about the Martian, I thought about how brave Amber had been, charging at the space alien, flailing her arms and acting like a crazy person. It had been a risky, gutsy move, but it had paid off and saved our lives.

"Keep your eyes peeled," I said as we continued making our way along the trail. "That thing could be hiding anywhere."

"What if he went to the campsite?" Tracy asked.

I hadn't thought about that. The crazed space alien would cause an awful commotion. People would be running around, shrieking and screaming, not knowing what was going on. There was no telling what would happen.

But we wouldn't have to worry about the maniac Martian showing up at the campground. To our left, there was a sudden explosion of noise: breaking branches and limbs, snapping twigs, and an unearthly, unintelligible gibberish-like wail.

The Martian had been waiting for us, right next to the trail.

We had been ambushed!

26

Tracy had been so surprised that she dropped her weapon and started running. Amber raised the gun and held it at her hip, pointing it at the space alien.

I wasn't going to take any chances. I swung the weapon around, placed the stock to my shoulder, and clicked the safety switch to the off position. When the Martian charged, I was ready.

I squeezed the trigger.

For a second, nothing happened, and I was gripped by a black horror. I had been certain that we'd solved the problem, that now that we knew about the safety switch, the weapons would work.

Not so.

I was about to drop the weapon and run when a sudden, enormous blast emitted from the barrel of the gun. A neon-green burst of light shot out like a death ray, hitting the maniac Martian square in the chest.

The effect was unbelievable. It didn't knock the creature over, didn't punch a hole through him, nothing like that. Rather, the entire creature turned to ice instantly! He was frozen solid!

For the billionth time that day, I was shocked into a stupor. I couldn't speak. The only thing I could do was gaze in amazement at the frozen Martian. The weapon in my hands suddenly took on new meaning, and I now realized how incredibly potent and deadly it was.

"Holy cow," Amber breathed. "You turned him into a block of ice."

My sister had returned to join us, and she, too, stared at the frozen creature standing in the woods several feet from the trail.

"Will it wear off?" Tracy asked.

I shook my head. "I don't know," I said. "But I don't think so. I think once you get turned to ice, you're pretty much done for."

Bravely, I took a few steps toward the frozen Martian, slowly reaching out my hand until my fingers touched his arm. He was very cold, shiny, and wet.

"He's already started to melt," I said.

"Wow," Tracy said.

"Another reason why you probably shouldn't take that to school," Amber said. "If your teacher gives you a bad grade, you're liable to turn her into a block of ice."

I almost laughed out loud. While it might be funny to see my teacher, Mrs. Dawkins, turned into an ice sculpture, she was very nice to me, and I wouldn't want to do anything to hurt her.

"At least we know we'll be able to make it back to the campsite," I said. "With these guns, I think we'll be unstoppable if we happen to get attacked by any more maniac Martians."

We had just started walking when a sudden cloud in the sky created a shadow on the ground around us. It drifted over us so quickly that it seemed unnatural and strange. I turned and looked up.

My jaw fell.

The rifle fell absently from my hands and dropped to the ground.

Amber gasped.

Tracy shrieked.

I could only stare.

An enormous alien spacecraft was hovering over us!

Shocked.

Amazed.

Awestruck.

Mystified.

Horrified.

I felt all of those emotions and more as I looked up at the gigantic flying saucer hovering in the air not far above the trees. I was certain it was the flying saucer that had crashed in the field.

But that's impossible, I thought. *That spacecraft was torn wide open. There's no way they could have repaired the hull so fast. They may be Martians, and maybe they are even an advanced race, but nobody could fix the flying saucer that fast.*

Except for a faint hum, the craft made no sound whatsoever. It simply hung above us, rotating slowly. How it could remain in the air without crashing to the ground was a mystery. I knew how planes worked, I knew how helicopters worked, and everyone knows how hot air balloons work.

But the flying saucer above seemed to be floating on its own, as if it were lighter than a feather.

Amber spoke.

"I've seen movies where this happens," she said. "And it never ends up good."

"Are . . . are we being invaded by Martians?" Tracy asked.

"I don't know," I said quietly. "All I know is that things will never be the same on Earth again."

Again, I thought of all those people I'd seen on television, the ones who claimed they'd been kidnapped by space aliens. I remembered how I thought they were probably the craziest people in the world, that they made up their stories just to get on television, just so they could write a book and sell a bajillion copies. I thought they just wanted to be famous.

Now, I realized I was wrong. It now made perfect sense. Martians—aliens from another planet—really are visiting Earth! I was seeing it with my own eyes, and as my dad says: *seeing is believing.*

And I was overcome by the strangest feeling. Although I tried to run, really, really *wanted* to run, my body just wouldn't listen. I told my legs to move, I ordered my feet to begin taking steps, but they wouldn't listen. It was like being wrapped in that weird plastic stuff the Martians used to seize us.

But this time, the only thing stopping me was my mind. I was too stunned to move. It was like being in a trance, in a nightmare from which I couldn't wake.

In the middle of the flying saucer, a small hole began to open up, exposing a shadowy interior. The hole opened wider and wider and then stopped. I could only assume that what lay beyond the hole was the inside of the flying saucer.

All at once, we were bathed in light. It wasn't as if a light shot down at us, as it happened much too fast. It was as if someone flipped the switch, and a tube of light turned on, connecting the ground and the spaceship.

And in that tube of light?

Three human beings. Three kids. Me, Tracy, and Amber.

The light was blinding, and I closed my eyes.

"Damon!" Amber shrieked. "What's going on? What's happening?"

Her voice seemed to break the spell in my mind. I was finally able to move, and I raised my hands to shield my face from the light pouring down on us.

"I don't know!" I replied. "I don't know, but we better get out of here as soon as we—"

My feet left the ground. I opened my eyes, squinting in the harsh light, only to see Tracy and Amber being pulled off the ground, too.

"Damon!" my sister shrieked. *"Damon! Help me! Help me! I'm being pulled into the air!"*

My sister was wrong. We weren't being pulled into the air, we were being pulled into the flying saucer . . . and there wasn't a single thing we could do about it.

Falling up.

It was probably one of the weirdest feelings I had ever experienced in my life. I kicked with my legs and flailed about with my arms, trying to find some sense of balance, but it was impossible. I was drifting, slowly, higher and higher, up toward the spacecraft, toward the hole in the middle to where we were ultimately being drawn.

And that very thought nearly scared me to death. I was powerless once again, just as I had been when I was wrapped up in that bizarre plastic, only this time it was a different type of helplessness. I was free to move about as much as I wanted, but nothing I did mattered. It was as if the laws of gravity had been repealed, or perhaps I no longer had any weight to my body. I felt as if I did, but I continued rising higher and higher, closer and closer to the monstrous flying saucer that hovered in the air above, slowly spinning just above the treetops.

My hand smacked into something: Amber's head.

"Ouch!" she said.

"I'm sorry," I said. "I didn't see you there. Give me your hand."

Amber reached out her hand, and I took it in mine. Tracy was nearby, and she was able to reach out and grab Amber's free hand. Then, we were all able to hold each others' hands as we rose together, three terribly frightened, completely horrified kids that had gotten into trouble far deeper than we ever could have possibly imagined.

No more was said as we continued to rise

higher and higher, closer and closer to the flying saucer. The opening now seemed like a large mouth waiting to devour us, and I hated to even think about what was waiting for us on the inside.

Finally, we reached the open portal and found ourselves inside the spacecraft. The portal door closed beneath us, and we were gently lowered until our feet touched the floor.

It was then that I realized this wasn't the same spacecraft that had crashed. Although it looked very similar on the interior, there were a number of things that were different, including the number of chairs near the front cockpit. And the metal walls were a different color, more coppery-gray than the other flying saucer.

The only things that were the same as in the other spacecraft were the beds near the far wall, beds with the same straps used to hold down humans while the Martians conducted their abominable experiments on poor, helpless individuals . . . like us.

Tracy, Amber, and I were still holding hands

as we nervously looked around.

"Where are they?" Amber asked. "Where are the Martians?"

As if hearing her, a large panel suddenly swept open, and four aliens appeared. They were identical to the Martians that had abducted us and taken us back to their flying saucer, except their suits were different colors. They approached us slowly, grim-faced and solemn.

It was as if I could read their expressions and their minds. As if I knew what they wanted, what they intended to do with us.

The gruesome experiments on our bodies were about to begin.

After everything that we'd experienced that day—seeing the spaceship trailing smoke in the sky, finding the alien craft, encountering Martians and being kidnapped by them, being taken aboard their vessel, stealing their guns and escaping, turning a Martian into ice, and then being pulled from the ground and brought into another alien spacecraft—well, I thought things couldn't get any stranger.

Until one of the Martians spoke to us.

In perfect English.

"Greetings, people of Earth," he said, and his voice was so shockingly human, so much like an ordinary person, that I flinched.

"You . . . you can . . . can speak English?" I stammered.

The Martian nodded, looking down at me. "Yes, person of Earth," he said, addressing me very formally and respectfully. "We can speak the languages of all humans on your planet."

"Are you going to probe my brain with a metal rod?" my sister asked.

Hearing this, the Martians looked at each other for a moment. Then, they all broke into uproarious laughter.

The Martian that had been speaking to me explained.

"No," he said, shaking his head from side to side. "Why would you think such a silly thing?"

"Because we see and read stories all the time about how humans have been abducted by aliens, brought aboard their flying saucers to have awful experiments conducted on their bodies," I replied.

"Do not worry," the Martian replied. "We come in peace. We are not here to harm you or any Earth person. In fact, this is the first time we have visited your planet, traveling millions of miles, and we have only done so for emergency purposes."

"What kind of emergency purposes?" Amber asked, and I was suddenly struck with the impossibly ridiculous notion of what we were doing at that very moment. We were actually in a Martian flying saucer, talking with aliens from another planet like they were our next door neighbors! Crazy.

But, then again, when you think about it, that was actually true. Being that they were from Mars, they really *are* our next door neighbors.

"Normally," the Martian said, "we would never come to your planet. The atmospheric conditions are not favorable for us, as the conditions on Mars would not be favorable for you humans. But we are here on an urgent mission, and we must complete this mission with great haste."

And as strange as it sounded, when he told us what that mission was, everything all began to make sense.

Everything.

"We are searching for one of our vessels that crashed on your planet," the Martian said. "We believe this happened very recently. However, the crash must have damaged the radio recovery transmission, as we have been unable to locate it."

"We know exactly where it is!" I said. "It's not far from here at all."

This caused much chatter among the Martians, but they were talking in their native language, and I couldn't understand what they were saying. When they calmed down, the Martian that had been conversing with us spoke.

"You say the craft is not far from here?"

Amber, Tracy, and I all nodded at the same time.

"It can't be more than a mile away," Amber said. "If you're flying around in this thing, I can't believe you wouldn't have found it by now."

"In an emergency, our vessels are equipped with invisibility shields to make it difficult for other alien races to find them."

"But it's not invisible," I said. "We could see the thing as plain as anything."

The big Martian nodded. "From the ground, you would have no difficulty seeing the craft. The invisibility shield is like a flat plate that rises above the spacecraft. The vessel would be easily seen from the ground. But from the air, it would be impossible to detect as long as the invisibility shield was in place."

That made sense, and it was actually pretty smart. If there was a report of a crashed flying saucer, the first thing the authorities would send out would be search planes. An invisibility shield like the Martian described would make the crashed flying saucer impossible to see from the air.

"Well," Tracy said, "we know exactly where it is."

"It would be most helpful if you could show us where it is located," the Martian said.

"But how?" I asked. "You said that we won't be able to see it from the air."

"We will return you to the ground and follow you to the vessel," the Martian said.

That made me really nervous.

"I'm not sure if that's a good idea," I said. "The Martians from the other spacecraft kidnapped us and wrapped us in plastic. I don't think they like us very much."

Once again, this prompted much Martian chatter among the space aliens.

"Please understand something," the head Martian said. "The atmospheric conditions on your planet are not meant for Martians. There is far too much oxygen in your air, and if we are exposed to it for too long, the effects can be mentally debilitating."

"What does 'debilitating' mean?" Tracy asked.

The Martian thought about this for a moment. "I guess you would say that the atmospheric conditions on your planet would make any Martian go crazy after a short period of time. That is why we must find the flying saucer and its crew as quickly as possible."

That's why the Martians were acting like maniacs, I thought. *Breathing the air on Earth was slowly making them go mad. Our air was turning them into maniacs.*

"But what about the Martian that we turned into an ice sculpture?" Tracy asked.

I winced. I wasn't sure if it was a good idea to tell them that we'd killed one of their own kind.

The Martian looked at Tracy. "Did you shoot him with a freeze ray?" he asked.

While I wasn't exactly sure what a 'freeze ray' was, I was certain that he must be talking about the guns we'd stolen from the crashed saucer.

I nodded sheepishly. "We didn't mean to," I said defensively. "We didn't have any other choice."

"He'll be fine," the Martian said. "The effect will wear off quickly. Freeze rays are meant to subdue an attacker only for a short period of time. There will be no long-term consequences."

That was a relief. I didn't know if he was going to be mad.

The Martians scattered throughout the spacecraft, busying themselves with whatever tasks were necessary. As for Tracy, Amber, and me, we found ourselves once again floating up off the floor of the vessel. It was the strangest feeling, hanging in the air, not attached to anything.

In the next instant, the portal beneath our feet began to open, and we could see the Earth below us. Light poured down upon us and struck the Earth, and we began a slow descent back to the ground. It was an unnerving experience, hanging in the air like that, and a bit horrifying. Still, I trusted that the Martians knew what they were doing and wouldn't let any harm come to us.

In less than a minute, we had returned to solid ground. The light vanished, and we were once again in the grip of Earth's gravity.

The guns we had stolen were still on the trail. I picked up the one I'd dropped, and Amber and Tracy did the same.

I looked up at the massive flying saucer looming overhead. The portal closed, but the spaceship remained where it was.

"Now what?" Tracy asked.

"I guess we hike back to the crashed flying saucer," I said. "They'll probably follow us."

"But what about that Martian that we froze?" Amber asked. "What if the effect has worn off?"

"Then, we'll have to freeze him again," I said. "You heard that guy in the flying saucer. The atmosphere on Earth makes Martians go crazy. At least with these guns, we can defend ourselves."

The flying saucer hummed above us. Birds in trees chirped, seemingly unaware or not caring about the massive craft hovering overhead.

But now there was another sound altogether, and I recognized it instantly.

The helicopter.

It was coming back, and fast.

Suddenly, it appeared overhead, just above the trees, so close that we could see the pilot sitting in the cockpit. He was wearing a headset, and he was staring up at the gigantic flying saucer with an expression of shock and disbelief.

But what was most disturbing was what happened next, something we could have never predicted.

Another portal opened beneath the spacecraft, and two long, large barrels emerged, aiming right at the hovering helicopter. They looked like the cannons on the deck of a military ship in the ocean. The helicopter pilot appeared dazed, too shocked at what he was seeing to even move.

"Oh, my gosh!" Amber exclaimed. "The Martians don't realize that the pilot doesn't mean to hurt them! They're going to blow the helicopter right out of the sky!"

As if waking from a terrible nightmare, the pilot suddenly realized that he was in extreme danger. The helicopter suddenly banked sideways and sped off, and the thumping of its blades began to fade as it vanished over the trees.

"Do you think they would have shot the helicopter?" Tracy asked.

"I don't know," I replied. "Maybe they did it just to scare the pilot away."

"It worked," Amber said. "I'll bet that's something the pilot will never forget."

We started walking, and it was impossible not to turn our heads every few seconds and look up at the flying saucer. It truly was an incredible sight.

Suddenly, I remembered my camera. I switched the freeze ray gun to my left shoulder and dug into my right front pocket.

"I forgot all about this!" I said, holding the camera. With one hand, I turned the camera on and aimed up at the spacecraft. I took several pictures, and they turned out perfect.

"Now we have proof!" I said. "And these won't be blurry and out of focus like all of the UFO pictures that we see in the newspapers!"

We passed the place where we used the freeze ray on the Martian, but we didn't see any sign of him. We remained wary, however, on the lookout for him or any of the other Martians that were, by now, probably looking for us. Thankfully, we didn't see any.

It didn't take us long to reach the field where the flying saucer had crashed. I looked up at the spacecraft looming above us in the sky and then pointed to the crashed vessel in the field. I didn't know if the Martians above would see me or whether they would even understand the gesture. But, apparently, they did, because the craft began to sink lower and lower, finally landing in the field in front of us.

"Get a picture of that," Amber suggested.

"Good idea," I said. Once again, I dug into my pocket, pulled out the camera, and clicked off a few pictures.

"What now?" Tracy asked. "Can we go home?"

"I suppose so," I said. "But they're probably going to want our guns. We should probably go give them back. I mean, I'd love to keep mine, but I don't want them mad at us.

"Plus," I continued, "I'd like to get some pictures of the Martians themselves. Then, we have absolute proof of alien life on other planets."

We started out toward the flying saucer that had just landed in the field. My thoughts were racing, and I couldn't wait to show my pictures to everyone, to tell my family and friends what we'd experienced.

We're going to be famous, I thought excitedly. *We're going to be in newspapers and on television and all over the Internet.*

I was so wrapped up in my thoughts of being famous that I'd completely forgotten something.

The space aliens that had kidnapped us.

The Martian aboard the flying saucer had told us that Earth's atmosphere wasn't good for them, and it made their kind get crazier and crazier the longer they were exposed to our air.

By now, the Martians that had crashed their flying saucer had been breathing Earth's air for several hours. It was enough to make them completely and totally crazy—crazy enough to launch an all-out assault. We had no idea that they were coming up behind us . . . until it was too late.

"Look at that!" Amber said as she pointed to a door that was opening in the side of the flying saucer that was in the air. It was identical to the door in the damaged spacecraft, but this one had an automatic staircase that unfolded to the ground. The gigantic Martians began pouring out, but their actions alarmed me.

They were running toward us! Not only that, they were carrying guns!

Tracy, Amber, and I stopped in our tracks.

"I don't think this is a good sign," I said

nervously. "Maybe they're not so friendly after all."

The Martians were shouting something in what sounded like English, but they were too far away for us to understand.

"I say we get out of here now," Amber said.

"I say you're right!" I said.

The three of us turned to run, shocked that there were even more Martians behind us! They, too, were running toward us, but they were shaking and trembling, waving their arms in the air, running in strange zigzags. Clearly, they had been breathing the air for too long. They had gone totally insane.

"They're all crazy!" Amber shouted. *"Every single one of them!"*

We did the only thing we could do: we raised the rifles to our shoulders and prepared to fire at the Martians that were coming up behind us. They were a lot closer than the other ones, and if we could freeze them first, then we could turn around and shoot the other ones.

That is, of course, if they didn't shoot us

first.

I switched off the safety and was just about to pull the trigger when I heard one of the Martians behind me shout.

"No!" he exclaimed. "Don't shoot! Get down on the ground!"

My instincts told me to ignore the Martian, but I obeyed him, anyway. After all: they hadn't done anything to hurt us, and we understood why the other Martians had acted the way they did. They'd breathed too much of our air. They didn't intend to harm us; in fact, they didn't even know what they were doing.

Amber, Tracy, and I fell to our knees and slumped to the ground. Both groups of Martians were surging toward us, but the ones that had emerged from the flying saucer began firing their weapons. Bursts of light—yellow, green, blue, and orange—flew over our heads, connecting with the crazed Martians that had been surging behind us. One by one, the maniac space aliens fell to the ground.

"They killed them!" Tracy said. "Why would they do that? I thought they came here to rescue them."

The firing stopped, and the Martians that had been acting so crazy were now sprawled over the ground, motionless.

The other Martians approached.

"Are you all right?" one of the Martians asked.

"Yeah," I said, getting to my feet. Tracy and Amber stood.

"Are they dead?" Amber asked, pointing to the Martians that were laying on the ground a few feet away.

"Not at all," the Martian replied as he shook his head. "They're unconscious. Now that they have been knocked out, we will be able to get them back into our craft where they will be able to breathe our Martian air. When they come to, they won't remember what happened."

We knew that we should probably be getting back to our campsites, but for the next half hour, we were fascinated as we watched the Martians carry the unconscious aliens to their flying saucer.

"I wonder what they're going to do with the crashed spacecraft?" Amber asked.

"They'll probably call for a spaceship tow truck," I snickered.

"Funny," Amber replied, shaking her head.

Actually, what they did was even more fascinating: after they'd carried all of the unconscious Martians into their saucer, we watched as yet another panel in the side of their craft opened. An enormous barrel emerged; the sort of barrel you'd see on a tank or on a battleship. It slowly swung around until it was aimed directly at the crashed flying saucer. At first, I thought the Martians were going to shoot a bomb or some sort of rocket to make the spacecraft explode, but that's not what happened at all.

Instead, a strange, white-yellow, jagged bolt—electricity, I presumed—leapt from the barrel and connected with the flying saucer. The bolt made loud hissing and popping sounds, and it twisted and turned like a mad snake. All the while, the electrical connection to the crashed craft was never broken.

Nothing seemed to happen for a long time, and I couldn't figure out what the Martians were up to.

"What are they doing?" my sister asked.

I shrugged. "Maybe it's going to blow up," I said. "The Martians probably don't want to leave it here for humans to find."

Amber's eyes lit up. "No!" she said excitedly. "It's not going to blow up! Look what's happening!"

We watched in total amazement at what was happening to the damaged flying saucer.

The spaceship was vanishing!

It was incredible, but true. The craft began to shimmer and waver, as if we were watching it through heat waves. Slowly, the flying saucer appeared to be turning into vapor!

"Wow," I whispered.

While we looked on, the spaceship became fainter and fainter, thinner and thinner. It took a couple of minutes, but soon, there was nothing left of the crashed flying saucer. It had completely vanished, leaving only a deep gouge in the earth.

We watched as the enormous barrel withdrew back into the ship, and the panel closed. Then, several Martians emerged from the flying saucer and strode over to inspect the area.

"They're probably making sure there's no sign of the ship," Amber said.

"But that gouge in the ground looks pretty unnatural," I said. "It looks like something crashed, like a meteorite."

The Martian that we were now familiar with, the one who had been talking with us, came out of the spaceship and approached us.

"They're going to be fine," he told us. At first, I didn't understand what he was talking about. Then, I realized he meant the other Martians. They had taken them to their spacecraft where they would be able to breathe the Martian air and return to normal. If you could call Martians normal, that is.

"Are you going back to Mars now?" I asked.

The Martian nodded. "Yes," he replied. "It is important that we leave your Earth as soon as we

160

can. We don't want humans to discover us for another few hundred years, when your species is a bit more mature."

I guess I was a little offended by that. What he was saying, basically, was that the human race is immature. But, then again, the more I thought about it, the more I thought that he probably was right. It would probably be best if the Martians left our planet without being discovered, at least for the time being. Humanity probably wasn't ready to be in contact with a race of highly intelligent beings from another planet.

The Martians that had been inspecting the crash site returned to the spacecraft. The one that had been talking with us continued to speak.

"We're sorry if we caused you any harm," he said, looking at Amber, then Tracy, and then me.

"We didn't get hurt," Amber said.

"We got super scared a couple of times," my sister said.

The spacecraft emitted a low, whirring sound, which grew to a heavy drone, then a roar.

The Martian turned and looked back at it, then turned and looked at us.

"Time to leave," he said. "Farewell, my Earth friends. Be well."

The three of us waived. We said nothing as the Martian turned and vanished into the spaceship.

"We should probably get away from that thing," I said, taking a few steps back. I raised my camera and took a couple of pictures, suddenly realizing that I didn't get any shots of the space aliens.

"Man!" I said. "I had the perfect opportunity to take a picture of one of those things, but I forgot!"

"That doesn't matter," Amber said. "You've got plenty of pictures of the spacecraft. That will be good enough."

Light began to flash on the flying saucer, and it slowly rose into the air. But instead of flying up in the sky, it moved over the crash site. Dozens of light beams shot straight down, and they began to move in a circular fashion in and around the hole that had been created by the doomed flying saucer.

"What are they doing that for?" Tracy asked. Amber and I didn't reply. We had no idea what they were doing.

However, within minutes, it became perfectly clear. The ground began to churn and move. In particular, some of the small hills that had been created when the spacecraft hit the ground and dug a hole were being knocked down, filling in the large gouge.

Quickly, I took a few more pictures, checking the viewfinder to make sure they came out okay.

"They're covering their tracks," I said. "They're going to repair the crash site and make it look like nothing ever happened."

And that's exactly what they were doing. After a couple of minutes, the hole was gone. The ground still looked disturbed, like someone had dug a hole and refilled it. No grass grew where the spacecraft had crashed, but I was sure it would grow back in time. No one would have any idea that an alien spacecraft had crashed in the field. The Martians would return to their planet, and no one would know except us—and we had the proof. I had pictures on my camera that would show the world absolute proof of our Martian encounter.

The spacecraft began to rise and spin. More lights began to flash. I clicked off several more pictures . . . and that's when I noticed something else in the sky. Amber saw it, too, and her arm shot out. She pointed and gasped.

"Look!" she exclaimed. "Airplanes!"

I shook my head. "Those aren't airplanes!" I said. "Those are fighter jets! They're going to blow the flying saucer right out of the sky!"

The jets roared overhead, high in the sky. Then, they turned and dropped to a lower altitude, making another approach.

Meanwhile, the flying saucer continued to rise higher and higher. The two fighter jets made a wide circle around it.

"Do you think they're going to shoot at it?" my sister asked.

"I don't know," I replied. "I hope not."

"They might think that we're being invaded," Amber said. "They might want to shoot the flying saucer before it can reach a city."

They would never get the chance.

Without any warning whatsoever, the spacecraft shot straight up into the sky with such incredible speed that, within seconds, it was only a small dot. Then, it was gone. In mere moments, it had left our atmosphere and entered into the void of space, on its way back to Mars.

"Holy cow," Tracy said breathlessly. "That thing can go a million miles an hour."

The fighter jets continued to circle, as if they were confused. They spiraled higher and higher into the sky, searching for the spacecraft, but I knew that they would find no sign of it. The Martians were gone. Soon, after more circling and searching, the fighter jets were gone, too.

Now that our ordeal was over, I couldn't wait to get back to our campsite.

"Let's go back," I said. "I can't wait to tell Mom and Dad about what just happened."

"Me, too," Amber said. "It was a good idea to bring your camera. Now, we have absolute proof that we were visited by aliens from another planet."

"Let me see your camera, Damon," Tracy said. I handed it to her, and she turned it on and began scrolling through the pictures. Amber and I looked over her shoulder, watching each scrolling image as it flashed onto the screen. A couple of the pictures were blurry, but most of them were very clear.

"How do you get this thing to zoom in?" Tracy asked as she fiddled with a couple of buttons.

"Just press that small arrow button," I said, pointing.

"This one?" she asked.

She pressed a button, and a message flashed.

Delete all images?

"No! Tracy!"

I reached out to grab the camera from her hand, but it was too late. She had already pressed the *Enter* button. A little hourglass appeared for only a few seconds, then vanished. It was replaced by a dark screen and another message.

No images.

"Tracy!" I exclaimed angrily, grabbing the camera from her hands. "I can't believe you did that! You just erased all of the pictures!"

Tracy looked dumbfounded. "I didn't know!" she pleaded. "I didn't mean to! Honest! I was just trying to zoom in on one of the pictures."

I looked at the blank screen of the viewfinder.

No images.

We had no pictures, which meant we had no proof.

"Nobody's going to believe us now," I said, with resignation. "We don't have any proof."

"Yes, we do," Amber said. She pointed at the patch of disturbed ground in the field. "Right there," she said. Then, she pointed into the sky. "And don't forget," she continued, "those fighter jets saw the flying saucer, too. We might not have proof, but there are other witnesses who saw what we saw."

Amber was right. The fighter jet pilots certainly saw the spacecraft as it rose into the air and shot into the sky, vanishing high above. There might be other people who saw the flying saucers, too. There would be other people who could confirm our story.

"I'm sorry," Tracy said as tears formed in her eyes.

"It's okay," I said. I was still mad at her for deleting the pictures, but I knew she didn't do it on purpose.

We headed across the field and picked up the trail, chatting the entire way. It never even occurred to us that the Martians might have left one of their own behind . . . until something huge sprang from the bushes next to the trail and leapt in front of us . . . .

I must admit, the first thing I thought of when the creature leapt from the bushes was that it was a Martian. Certain of it, in fact.

That's not what it turned out to be. It turned out that we surprised a deer that had been sleeping. She must have awoken confused and disoriented, because she leapt into the middle of the trail and stood for a moment, watching us. She was only a few feet away.

Then, in sudden realization, she sprang again, leaping off the trail and quickly vanishing into the thick forest.

My heart was pounding, but I started laughing.

"I thought that was a Martian!" I said. "I thought he had been left behind, and he was going to attack us!"

Amber, too, was now laughing, and so was my sister.

"I did, too!" Amber said. "I'm glad it wasn't, though. We would've never gotten away."

We returned to the campsite without any trouble. Mom and Dad were sitting in lawn chairs, eating sandwiches. Amber was still with us, as we wanted to introduce her to our parents.

"There you are," Mom said. "We were beginning to think you guys got lost."

Tracy and I were so excited that we both started talking at the same time, chattering like crazy chimpanzees.

Dad started laughing. "One at a time, one at a time," he said. "Now: what's all this about flying saucers and Martians?"

We calmed down enough to explain everything that happened to us. Even Amber did a little talking, explaining some of the details. All the while, Mom and Dad listened to us with grins on their faces. It was obvious they didn't believe us.

If only Tracy hadn't erased those pictures, I thought. *Then, they'd have to believe us.*

"I don't know where you get these crazy ideas," Mom said.

"After battling those maniac Martians," Dad said, "you guys must be hungry. Maybe your friend would like a sandwich, too."

"But didn't you hear the flying saucer in the sky?" Tracy asked.

Mom and Dad shook their heads.

"What about the fighter jets?" I asked. "You must have heard them!"

Dad nodded. "I heard some jets go by," he said.

"They were after the flying saucer!" I insisted.

"Sure, they were," Dad said. He rolled his

eyes, and I knew right then there was no way he was ever going to believe us. We gave up trying to convince him, as we knew there was no way he or Mom would believe that we had been kidnapped by Martians and then escaped. They would never believe a flying saucer crashed in the field or that another spacecraft showed up to rescue the stranded Martians. No matter what we said, they thought we were just making up a story . . . until the police arrived later that afternoon.

Amber had gone back to her campsite. Mom was reading a book, and so was Tracy. Dad was talking with one of the neighboring campers about computer programming. As for me? I had found a stick, and I was attempting to whittle a miniature canoe with my pocket knife. So far, it wasn't going very well.

By then, Tracy and I had given up our attempts to get Mom and Dad to believe our story about the flying saucers and the Martians. They would never believe us, and that was that.

The sound of crunching gravel caught my attention, and I lifted my head and stop whittling. Two police cars stopped in front of our campsite.

I looked around. It seemed like everyone had stopped what they were doing and were now looking at the two blue vehicles. While we looked on, a single uniformed officer emerged from each car. They looked around, then approached my dad.

"Looking for someone, officer?" my dad asked.

Both police officers nodded their heads. "Actually," one of them said, "we were wondering if you folks saw anything earlier today."

I looked at Tracy, and she looked at me. Both of us knew right away what the police officer was talking about.

The other police officer spoke. "We're wondering if anyone saw anything strange earlier today," he said. "Something in the sky, perhaps?"

Mom and Dad looked at Tracy and me. We leapt to our feet.

Finally! I thought. *Someone else saw*

something and reported it to the police! Mom and Dad will have to believe us now!

Once again, my sister and I spewed out our story from beginning to end. We told the police officers how we'd discovered the crashed spaceship, how we'd been kidnapped but escaped, and how the other flying saucer had arrived. We told them that we went on board their spaceship and talked with them. We told them everything we could remember.

When we finished, the police officers looked at us. Then, they looked at each other.

Suddenly, as if they'd finally gotten the punch line to a joke, they both burst out laughing so hard I thought they were going to fall over.

"Yeah," one of the officers said, "that's kind of what I thought. Martians. You just can't trust 'em."

They didn't believe us, either!

"We had a report of some strange things in the sky," the other officer said. He was still laughing, trying to get his words out. "The military took it serious enough to send up a couple jets. The pilots said they saw something, but they're not sure exactly what it was. We've been on a wild goose chase all day long, but so far, your story has been the best."

"But it's not a story!" Tracy insisted. "It really happened to us."

"Yeah, yeah, sure it did," the other police officer said. "Come on, Stu. Let's go get that cup of coffee and donut you promised to buy me."

And with that, the two officers returned to their patrol cars, turned the vehicles around, and left.

As the cars faded from sight, I turned and looked at Tracy. Tears were running down her cheeks.

"What's wrong?" I asked.

"Me," she replied. "If I hadn't erased the pictures on your camera, we would have proof. People would believe us."

She really felt bad, and I felt sorry for her.

"Don't worry about it," I said. "It's not that

big of a deal. In time, humans will discover that there really is life on Mars. Maybe then, people will believe us."

"Yeah," she said, "but that might be fifty years from now."

Tracy returned to her book, and I returned to my whittling. It wasn't long before Amber came back to our campsite. There was another girl with her. I put down the stick I was whittling and stood. Tracy closed her book and placed it on the ground next to her lawn chair.

"This is Kendra," Amber said. "She's from Colorado. Kendra, these are my new friends, Tracy and Damon. They were with me when we were kidnapped by Martians earlier today."

"You told her?" I asked incredulously.

Amber nodded.

"And you believe her?" Tracy asked, speaking to Kendra.

Kendra nodded. "Absolutely," she said. "Crazy things like that happen all the time."

"Wait until you find out what happened to

her," Amber said, pointing at Kendra. "You won't believe it."

"After today," I said, "I'll believe just about anything."

"What happened to you?" Tracy asked Kendra.

"My friends and I were attacked by crickets," she replied.

I burst out laughing. "Crickets?" I said, choking on my words. "You have to be kidding me! Crickets are just little bugs!"

Kendra shook her head. "You know what the word 'carnivorous' means?" she asked.

I thought for a moment. "I think so," I replied. "Carnivorous means 'meat-eating.' A carnivore is an animal that eats meat."

Kendra nodded. "You're exactly right," she said.

"Wait a minute," I said. "Crickets don't eat meat. They eat plants."

"That's where you're wrong," Kendra said. "You see, these weren't ordinary crickets. They were carnivorous, and they were gargantuan." As she said this, she spread her arms wide.

I looked at Amber. "Did she tell you about this?" I asked her. "About carnivorous crickets?"

Amber nodded. "Yes," she said. "I believe her, and when you hear what happened, you will too."

And so, the four of us sat around the campfire, and Kendra began her incredible—and horrifying—story . . . .

Next:

#36: Carnivorous Crickets of Colorado

Continue on for a FREE preview!

1

When most people think of the word 'carnivore,' they tend to think of vicious, meat-eating creatures, such as dinosaurs or tigers. Or sharks, killer whales, polar bears . . . any number of animals around the world that prefer eating meat over plants. After all, that's what the word carnivore means: any animal that eats meat.

But *crickets?*

No one—including myself—would ever think of tiny crickets as dangerous predators. Crickets are just harmless, little insects that make soothing, chirping sounds by rubbing their wings together. Some crickets chirp during the day, some chirp all night long. They eat vegetation, not meat.

And there are different kinds of crickets: camel crickets, bush crickets, ant crickets, spider crickets, sand crickets, and more. In some countries, crickets are considered a delicacy, and people actually *eat* them! That just seems *so* gross. You would never catch me eating an insect in a million years. I don't care if I was starving. Just the thought of putting a bug in my mouth and chewing it up makes me want to puke. Yuck.

Most people in America are familiar with common field crickets that are found just about everywhere. These are small, shiny, black crickets that usually get no bigger than an inch. They're harmless. Field crickets are tiny and innocent and have never posed a threat to human beings. There has never been a good reason to be afraid of average, ordinary field crickets . . . until one horrifying day last summer in Aspen, Colorado.

But it had nothing to do with harmless, little

crickets. No, the madness that began that horrible day wasn't because of small, chirping insects. It was caused by gigantic, predatory monsters— enormous field crickets of huge proportions—all brought about by an experiment that went horribly, horribly wrong.

2

My name is Kendra Delaney, and I live in Aspen, Colorado. Although I've lived here all of my life and I've been to only a few other states, I can tell you that Aspen is probably one of the prettiest places in the United States. Sure, there are many other great places in the country. But Aspen has everything that I love: mountains, forests, rivers, streams, and lakes. The people are very friendly and nice.

But best of all, Aspen has snow. Tons and tons and tons of snow. Not all year, of course.

However, during the winter, it's common to get several feet of snow and even more farther up in the mountains.

Which is one of the reasons why Aspen is one of the most popular skiing destinations . . . not only in the country, but in the world. People come from all over to ski the fresh, powdery snow and take in the beautiful, majestic surroundings of Aspen.

I'm a great skier and snowboarder. My dad taught me how to do both when I was very little, so skiing and snowboarding are as natural to me as walking or running. Winter, as you can imagine, is my very favorite time of year. Oh, there's nothing wrong with summertime. I like the warm weather, hiking in the woods, and swimming in the pool, lakes, and rivers.

It's just that I love winter so very, very much. All summer long, I look forward to our first snowfall. I look forward to the ski resorts opening up. I look forward to wearing my cold-weather gear and hanging out with my friends on the slopes.

But there is another reason altogether why I like winter better than summer. Winter is the time when the animals hibernate, the time for insects to go away. But spring always follows winter, and summer follows spring . . . which means the return of mosquitoes, bees, grasshoppers, houseflies, and all sorts of other insects.

Including crickets.

I know it sounds silly, but just the sound of that word—*crickets*—makes my blood turn cold and my skin turn to ice. I imagine you would feel the same way, too, if what happened to me happened to you.

Looking back, I should have known that something was wrong in July of last year. Two of my friends—Kiersten Cooper and Bryson Hatfield—and I had been hiking in the woods on a trail near our house. The trail winds through a thick forest, but there are also sections of rock that jut up into the air like canyon walls. The path passes by an old abandoned farm with several barns and a large pasture. Never before had we seen anyone in or around the old farm.

Until one day last July.

Bryson was the first to see something unusual, and he stopped walking. I was right behind him, followed by Kiersten, and the two of us stopped, too.

"Look at that," Bryson said.

Kiersten and I stepped around Bryson to have a look. In the driveway of the old abandoned farm was a big box truck about half the size of a semi-trailer. It sort of resembled a giant, square bug, with a white cab for its head and a white block for its body. On the side of the box was a cartoon character of a large, black cricket. Above the insect were the words

Carpenter's Cricket Farm
Crickets for Any Purpose

"What does that mean?" Kiersten asked. "I

mean . . . what do you use crickets for?"

Bryson shrugged. "My dad uses them for fishing bait," he said. "He usually buys them at the sporting goods store. I guess I never thought about where crickets came from."

"That's it, then," I said. "They're probably going to raise crickets and sell them to sporting goods stores, so they can sell them to fishermen."

At the time, it seemed a little strange that someone would try to raise crickets in Aspen, Colorado. I guess I just figured that the cold weather would kill the crickets in the winter, and I thought that there might be other places in the country that would be better to raise insects, somewhere warmer, like maybe Arizona or California. Or maybe some of the southern states like Mississippi, Alabama, or Georgia.

While we watched, a man walked to the back of the truck. He raised a large door that rolled up, and what we saw made our jaws drop.

Inside the truck were two *gigantic* crickets, nearly as tall as the man himself!

3

The three of us were spellbound, horrified, and mystified.

"*Holy cow,*" Bryson breathed. "*Look at those things.*"

However, after a moment, we realized what we were seeing. The crickets weren't alive; they were simply large replicas of insects. While we watched, the man called to yet another man who came to his assistance. Together, they pulled out a ramp stowed away beneath the truck and carefully carried the two monstrous insects out of the white box, placing the motionless, giant bugs in the grass. Now that they were out of the truck and in the open, we could see that the characteristics of the insects were over exaggerated and cartoon-like.

"They must be using them as advertisements," Kiersten said.

"I'd like to have one of those in my front yard," Bryson said. "Could you imagine what people would think when they drove by? At a glance, those things look real."

I laughed. "Yeah," I said. "That would be pretty funny, all right."

Just then, one of the men turned and looked in our direction. I waved, and the man waved back.

"Let's go and say hi," I said, and the three of us began walking again.

When we arrived at the truck, the two men were leaning against it, resting. Nearby, the two gigantic cricket statues glistened in the sun.

"Hi," I said, waving my hand.

"Hello," one of the men said. He was wearing blue jeans, a red T-shirt, and a white baseball cap.

"Are you moving in?" Bryson asked.

The man with the baseball cap nodded. "That's right," he said. "Still have a lot of work to do to get the place ready, though."

Kiersten pointed at the two enormous cricket statues. "Are you guys opening a cricket farm?"

The other man was wearing brown overalls with a white T-shirt. He had thick, long, dark brown hair pulled into a ponytail.

"Right again," he said. "I'm Bill Carpenter, and this is my brother, Brad."

Brad, wearing a baseball cap, nodded.

"Are you raising crickets so you can sell them?" I asked. I know it seemed like a silly question, but I was still a bit mystified as to why someone would have a cricket farm in Colorado.

Bill Carpenter nodded. "We've been raising crickets our entire life," he said. "We sell them to sporting goods stores and pet stores."

Bryson frowned. "Pet stores?" he said. "People have crickets for pets?"

Bill and Brad Carpenter erupted into laughter.

"No, no," Brad said, shaking his head. "We sell them to pet stores, and they sell them to people who feed the crickets to their pets."

Again, Bryson frowned. "You mean dogs and cats eat crickets?"

Once again, Bill and Brad broke into a fit of laughter.

"Of course not," Bill said. "But lots of people have exotic pets like lizards, iguanas, snakes, and tarantulas. They need to eat, just like any other pet."

I guess I'd never thought of that. But, then again, I've never had a pet like that. We have a cat named Spaceman, and all we feed him, of course, is cat food.

Kiersten pointed to an address and a telephone number on the side of the truck. "Is that where you're from?" she asked. "Louisiana?"

Bill and Brad nodded. "We still have an operation in Baton Rouge," Brad answered. "But we want to try an experiment, and we need a location that has colder temperatures for five or six months out of the year."

"And Aspen seemed like the perfect place," Bill continued. "The summers here are warm, and the winters are cold with lots of snow. That's what we need for our experiment."

I was just about to ask another question, but Kiersten beat me to it.

"What kind of experiment?" she asked.

Bill and Brad looked at each other. They seemed reluctant to speak. Finally, Brad replied.

"Well," he said, "we just can't say right now. Cricket farming is a competitive business, and we don't want any of our competitors to find out what we're up to. If our experiment works, we'll have the biggest cricket farming operation in the country, and quite possibly the entire world."

"We'll be famous," Bill said, with a proud nod.

While we had no idea what their experiment was all about, we would soon learn one thing for sure: it was going to backfire in the worst way imaginable . . . and it wouldn't be long before Kiersten, Bryson, and I were in a battle with giant insects, fighting for our lives.

ABOUT THE AUTHOR

Johnathan Rand has been called 'one of the most prolific authors of the century.' He has authored more than 75 books since the year 2000, with well over 4 million copies in print. His series include the incredibly popular **AMERICAN CHILLERS, MICHIGAN CHILLERS, FREDDIE FERNORTNER, FEARLESS FIRST GRADER,** and **THE ADVENTURE CLUB.** He's also co-authored a novel for teens (with Christopher Knight) entitled **PANDEMIA.** When not traveling, Rand lives in northern Michigan with his wife and three dogs. He is also the only author in the world to have a store that sells only his works: **CHILLERMANIA!** is located in Indian River, Michigan and is open year round. Johnathan Rand is not always at the store, but he has been known to drop by frequently. Find out more at:

www.americanchillers.com

Johnathan Rand travels internationally for school visits and book signings! For booking information, call:

1 (231) 238-0338!

www.americanchillers.com

JOIN THE FREE AMERICAN CHILLERS FAN CLUB!

It's easy to join . . . and best of all, it's FREE!
Find out more today by visiting:

WWW.AMERICANCHILLERS.COM

And don't forget to browse the on-line superstore, where you can order books, hats, shirts, and lots more cool stuff!

ATTENTION YOUNG AUTHORS!
DON'T MISS

JOHNATHAN RAND'S

AUTHOR QUEST

THE DEFINITIVE WRITER'S CAMP
FOR SERIOUS YOUNG WRITERS

If you want to sharpen your writing skills, become a better writer, and have a blast, Johnathan Rand's Author Quest is for you!

Designed exclusively for young writers, Author Quest is 4 days/3 nights of writing courses, instruction, and classes at Camp Ocqueoc, nestled in the secluded wilds of northern lower Michigan. Oh, there are lots of other fun indoor and outdoor activities, too . . . but the main focus of Author Quest is about becoming an even better writer! Instructors include published authors and (of course!) Johnathan Rand. No matter what kind of writing you enjoy: fiction, non-fiction, fantasy, thriller/horror, humor, mystery, history . . . this camp is designed for writers who have this in common: they LOVE to write, and they want to improve their skills!

For complete details and an application, visit:

www.americanchillers.com

All AudioCraft books are proudly printed, bound, and manufactured in the United States of America, utilizing American resources, labor, and materials.

USA

208